Hornet's Nest

Also by Bart Moeyaert:

Bare Hands

Hornet's Nest

Bart Moeyaert

translated by
David Colmer

Front Street
Asheville, North Carolina
2000

Printed in the United States of America

First edition
Designed by Helen Robinson

This edition was produced with the support of the
Administration for Art of the Flemish Community.

Library of Congress Cataloging-in-Publication Data

Moeyaert, Bart.
[Wespennest. English]
Hornet's nest/ by Bart Moeyaert ; translated from the
Dutch by David Colmer.
p. cm.
Summary: An attractive young puppeteer's visit to a small
European village inspires fourteen-year-old Susanna to try to
solve a neighborhood dispute over noisy dogs.
ISBN 1-886910-48-0 (alk. paper)
[1 City and town life—Fiction. 2. Puppet theater—Fiction.
3. Dogs—Fiction.] I. Colmer, David, 1964- ill. II. Title.
PZ7.M7227 Ho 2000
[Fic]—dc21
99-462093

Hornet's Nest

"Tell him it's coming."

My mother needed another pair of hands to hold me tight inside her and support her own back at the same time. She fell onto one knee, then the other, wrestled our front door open, and called out to Walda—who was four and playing with her dolls on the square.

"Walda!" she called, and her voice broke. "Run up the hill, will you? Run up to Wester's. Get Mr. Dantine. Tell him ..." She clenched her teeth—so hard it made her eyes water—and clung to the door as if she was about to tumble into a crack in the earth.

Walda stared open-mouthed at my mother. She had all kinds of questions, but my mother shooed them away.

"Tell him the baby's on its way!" she said and gulped for air like a fish in a bucket. "Tell him it's coming."

Walda took a step back. "It's coming," she repeated slowly, as if she wasn't quite sure what was supposed to be coming. "It is," she said. "It's coming."

She dropped her dolls, turned, and ran as fast as she could across the square, past the store that sold everything, over the lawn next to the church and up the hill, hugging the wall that curved around the graveyard.

"It's coming," she whispered. And again, "It's coming!" Her feet plowed through the mud on the city folks' hiking path, and halfway up she dove through a hedge. She zigzagged across the field. There were cows and cow pies. Grass lashed her ankles.

When she got to the Wester farm, she started screaming with all the breath she had left.

"Mr. Dantine! Mr. Dantine! It's coming!" Cackling chickens scattered to the corners of the yard. Walda almost tripped over one that wasn't fast enough, recovered, stumbled the last few steps, pounded on the door of the house, and called out again, "Mr. Dantine! It's coming!"

Up in the paddock the stable door flew open. Walda saw a man come out. She recognized him as my father and got so excited she started jumping up and down. She thought it was a new kind of game, something like red rover. When you heard your name, you had to run.

"It's coming!" she called again.

My father ran across the paddock. He held his coat shut to keep it from flapping.

"What about the cow, Dr. Dantine? The cow!" Wester shouted from the stable door.

"Let her loose!" yelled my father over his shoulder. He hurdled the hedge, grabbed Walda by the arms, and turned her into a shoulder bag.

"Child," he panted, and sprinted to the side of the house where his car was parked. He threw his stuff onto the backseat, threw Walda in on top of it, and jumped in behind the steering wheel.

"Hold tight!" he said. Our car took off down the dirt road. The motor screeched.

"Walda?" asked my father, after looking around everywhere at once without actually seeing anything. "Walda, was Mrs. Dantine by herself?"

"Yes," said Walda.

"No Bock?"

"No Bock." Walda put a hand to her throat to hold her voice in place. She was scared because my father swore and swung the wheel hard to dodge a bump and a pothole. She hit her chin.

"Mrs. Dantine hurts too," she said, and her head clunked against the window.

"Hurts bad?" asked my father.

"Bad. She fell over."

My father swung the wheel again. The car skidded around the corner and onto the road that cuts through the orchard to Helen's. The roar of the motor drowned out the dogs, but after my father pulled in between the kennels and turned the key, they were surrounded by barking and whining. The dogs threw themselves against their cages and bared their teeth.

"Stay there," my father told Walda. He jumped out of the car and stopped where he was.

Helen was coming toward him from between the kennels. Her rubber boots slopped on her feet. Her gloves and apron were filthy.

"What's the matter? Where's the fire?" she asked.

"The baby's on its way," my father said. "Bock's gone to town, it's Friday. You're the only one who can help."

"Help? With what?"

"With the baby."

"With the baby?" Helen's voice shot up. Her arms went up as well, and her eyes got big. She looked from one glove to the other. "My God, I don't even know if I still can," she said.

"Nobody else can," said my father.

Helen walked past the car and looked back at my father over the roof.

"You can't be serious," she said.

"You never forget something like that," said my father.

Helen shook her head. She grumbled under her breath. It was too long ago—she didn't even know what babies looked like anymore—but meanwhile she'd taken off her gloves and untied her apron and was walking toward the house.

"There always used to be an obstetrician," she said. "How am I ..." Her voice disappeared behind the door.

My father held his breath. He was still worried. He waited. Walking back and forth and to and fro—as if he had to pace out the length of the car a hundred times. Helen stayed inside the house, more or less for hours. In his mind it was too late, I'd been born ages ago, I was already celebrating my first birthday. He stuck out his lower lip, puffed air up over his face, and looked down at his watch. When he looked back at the house Helen was coming out the door. Her apron had turned white. It was clean and white, her old uniform.

"Beep, beep," she said, and dove into the car next to Walda, whose mouth was hanging open again.

The car swung around in front of the house and drove off between the apple trees in a cloud of dust.

"Towels," said Helen, tapping impatiently on the back of the front seat. "Boil towels in big pots on the stove. Have you got them—towels, big pots?"

"I think so," said my father.

"Sheets, clean sheets?"

"Them too," said my father.

"Now we just have to pray," said Helen.

I already existed, but at quarter past four, on October 3, I existed for sure. I only had to scream once, and the whole village knew. The houses around the church are crammed in so close together that people didn't need to go outside to spread the news. It was passed on from window to window and from door to door. Amanda, the village's talking newspaper, spread the message past the church steeple. Fifteen minutes later, they knew it at Wester's and at Bruwaen's dairy, at Meerten's and at the pig breeder's up on the expressway: the handsome young vet's beautiful wife has had a daughter. The news even made it to Squire Volcker, who lived in the mansion with the walled garden: she's healthy, and her name is Susanna.

"Just over six and a half pounds," said Helen once the worst was over. She nodded at my crib. "A bouncing baby, like all of October's children. They've had spring and summer. They're strong enough for the winter."

She dabbed my mother's forehead with a damp towel and smiled. "Everything went well, thank God. Now I can have my say. Edith, having your first child at home is dangerous. Nothing beats a clean hospital bed with a nurse and an obstetrician standing by. They've got machines there in case something goes wrong. Look. You wanted to have it at home, and now you've had it at home."

My mother didn't answer. She had dark rings under her eyes, and there were strands of hair hanging down around her face. All she wanted was to sleep. Preferably with me in her arms and my father close by.

"Where's William?" she asked.

"He's gone," said Helen. "To town. To get Bock from his bridge club. And he wanted to fill out the forms for Susanna at the whatchamacallit office, you know, if he makes it to city hall on time. 'Susanna Dantine, six pounds nine ounces—and a pound of that's in her butt.' I'm not kidding, Edith. One whole pound in her butt. Bock won't waste any time on her, that child's as fit as a fiddle, from head to foot."

Helen smoothed out my blanket and walked to the bathroom smiling.

"A healthy baby like that," she said, washing her hands, "William will tell everyone he meets. And then they'll all wish him luck, and with all that luck, nothing will ever go wrong for you again."

Helen turned off the faucet. She heard the echo of her own voice and saw herself smiling at the mirror. She thought, Look at me smile. I straighten out the corners of my mouth, and see: I'm not smiling anymore. Now my mouth matches my eyes. Look how much I've shrunk. Look at my apron: too big. Look at my sleeves: too long. Look at my hands: skin and bone.

She averted her eyes and dried her hands. That movement petered out as well. Her breath caught in her throat.

"Edith," she said. "I just realized that my husband doesn't know where I am. Rudy wasn't home when William came by. He doesn't know I'm here."

"Give him a call," said my mother from the bedroom.

"No," said Helen. She let out a sigh. "Let him guess. I don't know where he is either."

She straightened her shoulders and raised the corners of her mouth before coming back out of the bathroom and walking over to my crib. She forced herself to croon tenderly.

"Ohhh!" she crooned. "If you ask me, there's another pound in her ears. For heaven's sake, Edith, have you seen the ears on this child?"

She looked at the big bed and saw that my mother had fallen asleep. She made a noise with her tongue and sat down on a chair next to my crib, determined to stay a few hours longer the way midwives always do. She folded a towel in half, yawned, and folded it in half again. Her eyes were looking for something nice to settle on. In the end, she laid a hand on the side of my crib.

Maybe only a minute went by. Maybe half an hour. Maybe Helen looked at me for even longer.

The sight of my father suddenly standing there in the darkening bedroom made her jump. He was still wearing his coat, and it felt like he was bringing in warmth.

"They asleep?"

Helen straightened up. "Yes. Both of them." She watched my father, following him with her eyes. She saw him bend over my mother and kiss her on the forehead. Then she saw him come over to my crib and stroke my cheek with one big finger.

She shivered. She tried to suppress a sigh, but didn't quite manage. She slid her chair over to my father and asked him if he wanted to sit down.

"No, thank you, Helen," he said.

"Maybe you don't," she said and sat down again.

The room grew very quiet. It was a beautiful quiet because I had been born, and my beautiful mother was sleeping like an angel, and my handsome father was looking at me.

Helen compared my mother and me, and then my father and me, and then said with a sigh that Rudy couldn't do it, just sit still and enjoy the silence of a baby. "Rudy's head is full of dogs. Big dogs. When they're little they make him nervous. If he could beat size into them, he'd beat it into them."

ONE

A scooter races across the square and past our house. The buzzing disappears on the other side of the village, like a bumblebee flying into another room.

My mother puts her fork down on her plate and sits up straight. She presses her lips together and looks at me.

Outside, sparrows are twittering. The heat hums. The buzzing comes back sounding like a tractor on a faraway farm, then gradually gets louder, comes closer, changes, and finally becomes the racket of a scooter driving onto the square, stopping, and staying there spluttering.

My mother pushes back her chair and hesitates. She looks from her plate to the window. She's closed the shutters to keep out the noonday sun.

"Who's that?" she asks.

I straighten up, but my mother shakes her head, taps the table, and says, "Stay there. Eat your lunch."

Sighing, I slump down on my chair and push back, making it scrape over the tiles.

"Hello!" calls someone outside, and the scooter roars. "Anyone there?"

"At this time of day," says my mother through teeth that are almost clenched. "What a nerve. Raising hell at this time of day. Listen to him reveling in it."

"Revving it," I say.

"Eat," says my mother.

I want to say something back, but I forget what it is right away because I'm imagining myself on a scooter. I race uphill at top speed, take the curve with brakes squealing, and tear back down the hill. The thought alone gives me the butterflies.

"Hello!" the voice outside calls again and roars with laughter.

"Scum!" hisses my mother. She's playing forkball with a pea. "A minute ago it was nice and quiet." She gets up and carries her plate and silverware over to the sink.

"Ah ..." I say, and leave this sentence unfinished as well. Ah, at least something's happening for once, that was what I wanted to say, but nothing's happening, nothing at all. Outside, the scooter has gone quiet. Or ridden off. I hold my breath to catch every sound.

"Don't miss it!" calls the voice suddenly.

My mother turns around. I follow her eyes. We're looking at the green shutters in front of the window.

"Come and see it while I'm here!"

From outside comes the rattle of roll-up shutters. Amanda from the village store, the talking newspaper, has come out to see what's happening. A window squeaks open in her attic where David the widower lives. And Carla's voice booms out from the other side of the square, "Walda, come and take a look at this!"

When I hear that—"Walda, come and take a look!"—a noise escapes my throat. The idea of Walda's mother calling her over; mine just about locks me up in a cupboard.

I get up from the table—"Susanna, sit down!"—and open the window. Before my mother's had a chance to say anything, I push aside the shutters.

Sunlight streams into the room. Across the square, up against the yellow front of the church, in a noonday sun so bright I have to squint through my eyelashes, a young guy is standing with his arms spread wide.

He looks like he's about to burst into song, but each hand is holding a piece of wood with a puppet dangling from it. One of the marionettes looks wild, with red hair and red clothes that make you think of Spain; the other one's a blushing wench in a peasant dress. The puppeteer is standing between them beaming. He bends forward—his long black hair falls in front of his face—and makes the two puppets walk toward each other.

He does it so well I can't help but laugh. Grinning, I lean out the window and see that I'm not the only one. Amanda, David, Carla, and Walda are watching with smiles on their faces. Dr. Bock is there too. He's standing in the middle of the square, a black patch in a sea of light.

"Two ladies," says the puppeteer. "Two serious ladies."

"Boring!" shouts Walda. She can't help it, her trapdoor is always flapping open when you don't want it to.

"Okay then," says the puppeteer without looking up. He makes the puppets dance. "Two seriously cheerful ladies."

Amanda grins at Carla up on her balcony and shouts, "It's about us!" She grabs her apron by one corner, holds up one fat arm, and does a lumbering pirouette. She dances like a bear, but she brays with laughter. Everyone brays. Even Dr. Bock, and he's a serious gentleman.

Silence falls when the puppeteer asks, "What happens now? What happens when these two meet?"

"They visit an old man!" calls old man David from his attic window. He's pulled up a chair so that he can rest his arms on the windowsill. Sitting up there like that he looks like a toad, an ancient toad.

"They go out somewhere anyway!" shouts the young man in front of the church, while making the puppets skip lightly down the steps.

"They go to Concordia," shouts Walda. "They go dancing at Concordia!" She's all of eighteen, but that doesn't stop her from crowing like an eight year old.

"Squeaky accordion music," calls Amanda with a blissful expression on her face. She thinks they still hold old-time dances at Concordia.

I look from one to the other. Each time my eyes linger on the marionettes. And on the puppeteer too, but never for long, he's gorgeous. So gorgeous that air starts bubbling up in my throat, and before I know it I'm leaning out the window shouting, "Just make something fun happen!"

"Good," I hear him reply. "Good," he tells me, and I glow with pride. I try to quickly come up with something else, but a hand on the back of my neck pulls me away from the window. My mother plants her hands next to the geraniums in the window boxes, leans out over them, and screams, "And that's enough!" Her voice booms out over the square, then dies away.

Almost dumbstruck, I stare at my mother's tensed-up back. "Mom!"

"Go take your act somewhere else!" shouts my mother. "Go find some tourists or something, but leave us in peace! In peace!" she snaps, while swatting away my hands as I try to pull her back in.

In front of the church, the puppeteer lets his arms droop, and the marionettes go down on their knees. He frees one hand, shades his eyes with it, and peers into the sun. He just looks, he doesn't answer, the way he's standing says enough.

Carla breaks the silence. In tones so cold they give me the shivers, she says, "Edith Dantine, you should hear yourself! Peace! You, talking about peace?"

The hiss at the end of the word hangs in the air and makes the square quieter than it already was.

"Mom, stop it," I whisper. "Don't start again, please!"

And thank you very much. It's pointless.

"My dear Carla," says my mother softly, but in a voice dripping with venom, "you should hear yourself. In my home, things are peaceful. But every time you open your mouth, we feel the draft over here and the teacups rattle in my china cabinet. And you have the nerve to talk about peace to me? Peace?"

The hissing sound floats over to the other side of the square, to the balcony Walda and Carla are standing on.

"I'm not talking about your china cabinet!" Carla shouts back. "I'm talking about the dogs."

The dogs.

There's no getting away from it. Every conversation ends up at the dogs.

I hope that my mother will now silently close the shutters. I've had enough of looking at the square. I've had enough of the voices.

"The poor boy's not hurting anyone," calls out Carla. "He's just putting on a show. Entertainment is what you call that, Edith Dantine. Fun, amusement, but maybe you've forgotten the meaning of words like that. He might have begun by barking, but it was only temporary." She grins sarcastically.

My mother has never stuck out a fight this long before. But she's already gasping for breath. Her whole body is trembling and her voice is a screech, "He's still noisy, my dear Carla."

"Nowhere near as noisy as the dogs," Carla calls back. "And not every day, either."

With a groan that sounds like a chair on a tile floor, I turn back to my mother. "Mom, stop it. It's embarrassing, it's so embarrassing ..." I could die, that's what I want to say, but my mother isn't listening.

She's more interested in what's coming out of Carla's mouth. "I don't understand you, Edith Dantine. Those lousy mutts would raise the dead, but you don't say a word about that. Everyone wants the dogs out of the village, but you keep quiet. You refuse to speak up. That's your right, but don't go shooting off your mouth when some kid puts on a show for people. You shoo away dogs, not people."

My mother smiles listlessly.

I grab her by the arm, but only for a second. I feel the air draining out of my lungs. In front of our house, near the church, the puppeteer has started packing. He puts his marionettes to bed in their bag. Quietly, as though he can't hear the voices. Now and then he looks up—at the store, where Amanda is standing with her hands on her hips waiting to see what happens, or at David, who's watching the square like it's a football field. He doesn't deign to look at Carla or my mother.

"He's leaving," I say to no one in particular. "See what you've done now, he's leaving."

His scooter is parked at the bottom of the steps. The puppeteer straps his bag on the back and wheels the scooter out of the square.

I throw the dishcloth into the sink and run out of the kitchen, down the hall, and out the front door. Just in time to see him disappearing around the corner.

The noise of his scooter shuts everyone up. Carla and my mother stare at each other silently, Carla from up on her balcony—which strengthens her position— and my mother from our ground-floor kitchen window.

With imploring eyes, I look to Amanda for help, but she turns, shakes her head, and waddles inside. She's got her scoop for the day, it's time for her to open her store and tell the first customer who happens to wander in.

Everyone follows her example. David closes his

window. Dr. Bock walks on. Carla disappears inside her house. And my mother decides to slam the shutters.

"They're shut alright," says Walda up on the balcony.

I look up—meanly, I hope—and at the same time I act as if she leaves me cold.

Walda is not impressed. She laughs in my face. At least that's what I think first, but behind my back I hear the person who really makes her laugh. My mother has come out. She slams our front door, even harder than the shutters, and Walda suddenly laughs out loud. She pretends to be scared of my mother.

My mother doesn't let it get to her, either that or she doesn't notice. She strides past me across the square.

She stops at Carla's front door. She leans on the wall with one hand and puts the other one on her hip. It takes me a while to realize that what she's actually doing is pressing the bell for an outrageous length of time. She turns around and sees me standing there. She feels Walda's eyes on her and looks up.

"Is she going to let me in or what?"

In the same instant, the front door swings open. Carla takes position on the doorstep.

"Enough is enough," says my mother. Without waiting for an invitation, she pushes Carla's arm out of the way and goes inside.

Before I've had time to get over the shock, the door closes behind her.

"No," I whisper.

"Unbelievable," says Walda. She points at the open balcony doors with her chin. She raises her eyebrows and holds a hand over her mouth, as if that's the only way she can keep from laughing. "Unbelievable!"

The blood drains from my cheeks. High, agitated voices are audible out on the square. Snippets of words, half-screamed sentences. My mother and Carla are deaf to each other inside there. Burning with embarrassment, I look around to see if anyone else is out on the square listening. Amanda is in front of her store, I could have guessed. My legs are buckling, the ground's getting ready to swallow me. I try to pick up the words from inside, to make them out, to understand, but I can't think.

Walda is beaming, she's growing before my eyes. She shakes her head and bunches up her hair.

"Poor thing," she says.

Inside, someone is crying. I know the sound of my mother in tears, she cries often enough. I don't want to ask Walda a thing, the humiliation is too much to bear.

With her back to me and her arms spread, she leans up against the balcony doors.

"They're talking," she says. "They're talking."

"What about?" I'm immediately sorry I asked.

"About them good ol' days."

"What do you mean, them good ol' days?" My voice has almost had it. I dig my nails into the palms of my hands. "Walda, what are you talking about?"

"Be quiet, I can't hear a thing," she says. "Your mother's going to have some coffee. They're having a nice chat about your old days and my old days and—um—about Helen's dogs."

"Helen and the dogs," I say.

"Helen's dogs."

"They're not Helen's dogs. They're Rudy's dogs."

"What's the difference? They still have to go. By force if necessary."

"You sound just like your mother."

"You ... don't ... any ... more." She puts the words together carefully and snickers.

"My mother and I," I say, "my mother and I know very well why we stick up for Helen."

Walda grins.

"Really?" she nods. "Did you just say 'my mother and I'? Did you say 'we'?"

She comes over to the railing and leans on it with her elbows. "If you do something by yourself, you use the word 'I'. Not 'we'. Just a minute ago, over a cup of coffee, your mother signed the petition. It seems you are now the only one sticking up for Helen and the dogs. Poor thing."

Walda nods, closes her eyes in the conviction that I will turn out all right in the end, and disappears into the house. Inside, she starts laughing, roaring with laughter, and I curse her, and call her mother everything under the sun as well, and mine's not an ounce better.

"You walked! You walked!"

My beautiful mother was crazy about "first … and then after." When my father was going out on his rounds and wouldn't be back until late, it was coat-case-kiss time. She would stand waiting by the door with me on her hip and Daddy's coat over one arm. His briefcase would be ready at her feet, so that my father could pull on his coat first, then pick up his case, then kiss my mother and me good-bye. After the kiss, she always wrapped her hand around mine, walked out the door with Daddy, and helped me wave until he was out of sight.

In time, I could set my clock by it. Coat, case, kiss—bye Daddy. In time, I was able to wave without my mother's help.

Then my legs started itching. I wrestled out of my mother's arms, slid down her body to the floor, and landed with my two feet on the ground. I stood there. I stood. I reached out to my father as if there were handgrips in the air between us and—like a baby rabbit coming out of the hutch—took my first step. And my second. And third.

My father, who was already walking to the car, turned around and could barely believe his eyes. Sounding very different from my mother, he whispered, "Easy now, easy does it," and slowly retraced his steps, hands stretched out to catch me. He saw that I was staying upright and burst out laughing, and when I fell against his legs and looked back at my mother a few yards away, he picked me up and threw me up in the air.

"You walked!" he shouted. "You walked!"

My mother probably gave a sour little smile. We had deviated from her routine. She bustled around my father and me like a jealous dog and picked me up the first chance she got, only to have to put me down again right away because I was kicking my legs and crowing and laughing even louder than my father. I crawled around on the ground and tried to stand on my head. I fell against my father's legs, and my mother said, "Careful!" but I wasn't listening and tried again, and fell again, and again my mother told me to be careful, but my father looked at me and didn't tell me to be careful. No, he told me to keep on trying. He said, "Two feet on the ground is just as hard as legs in the air."

TWO

A mob of children storms down from the main street.

The little Wester kid comes running around the corner wheeling his bike and almost goes flying. "The tent's coming!" he shouts. "The tent!" Four more boys follow in his wake. They're beaming, you could light a match off their cheeks. Their thin voices linger over the square.

The Wester kid grabs me with his sticky fingers. "The tent!" he pants. "They're bringing the tent!" He might be on another planet, but he drags me back down to earth. He wants to see me skip or dance or jump, but nothing could be farther from my mind. I break free and give him a quick backhand. Only Amanda notices. She shakes her head and jots it down in her newspaper.

Kids stream in from everywhere. They start jumping up and down on the lawn next to the church, and the ones on bikes ride round and round in circles, as if they're trying to show where the tent is going to be set up.

The drone of a tractor driving down from the main street drowns out their screams. The road is barely wide enough. A long pole is poking forward over the head of the driver.

The kids go wild. As far as they're concerned, the party has already started. They call for everyone to come out.

David opens his attic window. Lily from the folk dance club is almost too scared to cross the street. Father Drecht charges out of the church in shirtsleeves and slippers and starts directing the tractor like a traffic cop. He doesn't realize that Wester is already doing the same thing.

The tractor drives past a few feet away from me.

I only have eyes for my mother, who is coming out of Carla's with her head bowed. Behind Carla's and Walda's backs, she makes herself smaller than she is.

The trailer swings toward me. I see the heavy wheels, I realize that I should move out of the way, but it doesn't get through to me, not till Wester gives me a shove. He swears, tells me he's saved my life, then goes back to following the tractor.

After the trailer has been maneuvered onto the lawn, my mother and I are alone on the square. We're maybe five steps away from each other, but she acts as if I'm invisible, and I act as if she's invisible. But my eyes are blazing. My mother is melting, I can tell. She does her best to keep her chin up, craning her neck like she's trying to look over an imaginary wall.

On the lawn, the tent pole is pointing up at an angle

like a finger of warning. Soon it will be standing up straight. Then they'll open the giant umbrella and the tent will be ready in one, two, three.

My mother dares a quick glance in my direction and slowly wanders over toward me.

"I'd forgotten about the party," she says.

Bitch, I say inside my head. You're lying. Only yesterday you were complaining about how noisy today would be.

"I'm not thinking straight."

Lying bitch, I say—under my breath.

"How could I forget? August. The summer festival. How stupid of me!"

"Yes, very stupid of you," I say.

She wipes her forehead, giggles about how silly she is, and tries to play the easygoing mom with an arm around my shoulders. I almost bite it.

"Don't touch me," I say.

"We'll never get the tent up like this. We have to work together!" shouts Wester on the other side of the square.

"Together!" says Father Drecht.

"Susanna, what ...?" says my mother.

"What's wrong?" I say. "You're asking me?"

In a flash my mother's face changes. She knows what I'm talking about. The corners of her mouth sag, her shoulders droop. Suddenly she's shrunk again and is looking at me questioningly.

"What choice did I have?" she says.

"You could have just ignored them and their stupid petition," I say.

"And be chased out of the village along with the dogs?"

"Better than betraying a friend."

"Susanna, things couldn't go on like that. Don't you under —"

"No," I say.

"Hey!" shouts Wester. "Hey, you Dantines, stop gossiping and come and help! We're not going to get that pole up by wagging our tongues."

Everyone looks in our direction. Walda and Carla and Amanda are huddled together like conspirators.

My mother quickly slips on her mask. The poor widow mask. She walks over to the lawn with arms dangling and says, "I won't be any use, I don't have any muscles."

Everyone's waiting for me to come over too. I've never been very good at masks, but with a mother like mine you learn fast. I try a half smile.

Walda's wearing a whole smile, a real one. "The grown-ups pull, the kiddies push," she says. "Two guesses what you get to do," she says. She thinks it's a good one, especially since Wester has grabbed my hands and put them in place on the pole. Five pairs of children's hands are under mine, with my mother's on the other side. I'm the child and she's the adult. The thought alone is enough to make me growl with rage.

Lily from the folk dance club is standing off to one side as if she wants to keep time.

"On the count of three," she says. "One."

I look my mother straight in the eyes.

"Two!" calls Lily.

"I won't forgive you," I say.

"Three!"

Everyone's muscles are tensed. The grown-ups pull, the children push, and gradually the pole goes up. No one notices that I'm rebelliously pulling in the wrong direction.

The tent pole slips into a metal slot and stays upright. Wester tugs the rope loose. The ribs spring out a little. Wester ducks under the canvas, calls in the help of the other men, and together they open the giant umbrella. Everyone steps back out of the way, and the canvas spreads over our heads like wings. The lawn is suddenly shaded, a cool spot smelling of musty canvas. The kids have got a new playroom.

"What a racket," I say, just loud enough for my mother to hear. "Things were so peaceful here earlier this afternoon."

My mother plays deaf, of course, even if she's suffocating under the mask on her face. She walks off to fetch the canvas panels for the sides with Carla and the other women.

The pieces have to be lashed onto the umbrella. It's one of the jobs the men never bother with.

Wordlessly the women split up into pairs. One woman inside the tent, one outside.

My mother and I are left over. We're stuck with each other. The rope comes through the clip. Pull. The rope goes through the clip.

"Pull," I say. "I haven't got all day."

"That's no way to talk to your mother." She pulls

the rope and sticks the end through the next clip.

I pull the rope all the way through.

"Have you figured out how to tell Helen?" I say. My hands aren't doing what I want them to. It takes me a while to get the rope back in the clip.

"No."

"You are going to tell her?" I tug the rope viciously.

"Of course."

"And what do I say if she asks me? I'm going up to see her."

It's quiet on the other side. No rope comes. For a few seconds I stand there staring at the faded red canvas.

"Well? What do I say if she asks me?"

Still no reaction. Then I realize: she's walked off. I peek around the edge of the canvas, push it aside, and hear Amanda's voice—sweeter than normal—"Where are you off to, Edith?"

I see my mother walking away. She looks down at the ground, shakes her head, and brushes aside any other questions.

She's crying. When she pulls our front door shut behind her, the click is way too soft.

"Where does Little Red Riding Hood live?"

I learned to be nice. That you have to listen and think twice before you open your mouth—but never when it's full. I learned that you don't go digging for lost treasure in your nose. That sneaky farts are okay, and that when you want to scratch your bottom you should wait till no one's looking. That white lies are all right, and that swearing is too, as long as it's not on purpose. I got to know the boundaries. Not only of what was allowed or not allowed, but the real ones as well.

At first, the world was within the arms of my beautiful mother and my handsome father. The hollow between their bodies, early in the morning in bed.

My mother, who always had her nose in a book, read to me. When I was little, I often went out with my father and I was always seeing sick animals, so I wanted to hear stories with animals in them, but healthy ones, not sick ones my father had to make better first, and the fairy tales had to be told so that I played a role in them myself.

"Where does Little Red Riding Hood live?" I asked once.

"In the woods," answered my mother.

I saw the woods she meant later, when the boundaries were pushed back. Volcker Wood had always been like something out of a fairy tale for me. The lane that led through it was slightly sunken in the hard, dark earth, and as straight as a road in a field. Small, mysterious paths branched off it and always came out somewhere. One led to a summerhouse, but no one knew what it was doing there. People said it belonged to a castle that had never been built. Another path led to a rickety coop, where the gamekeeper bred pheasant for Squire Volcker. Once a year, at the end of September, the almost-tame hens would be released for the first shoot a week later. Beyond the summerhouse and the coop, it was all trees and thick undergrowth. Overgrown rhododendrons and other plants Little Red Riding Hood could live under.

For a long time I thought that the name Volcker Wood had something to do with folklore, with stories, with fairy tales. It was only later that I realized the name came from Volcker: Squire Volcker who lived in the mansion with the walled garden. The man I have only seen once in my life.

But I'm getting ahead of myself. I wasn't that old yet.

THREE

The little Wester kid shoots past on his bike. "Get it!" he screams. "Kick it!" He throws down his bike.

At once, a screaming mob of kids races past. They're screeching like seagulls. "Get it!"

They're not talking about a ball, I realize that instantly. With looks of horror on their faces, Walda and Amanda run out of the tent. I follow them, and immediately the sunlight crashes on top of me, pinning me to the spot. I clap a hand over my mouth.

Farther along, I see a tangle of children. They're swinging their arms, jabbing with their elbows, and lashing out with their feet, and the whole time screaming till they go hoarse. They're playing soccer after all, but the ball isn't round, it's a dog, and I know exactly where it comes from.

"Stop it," I mumble, and then again, "Stop it!" The sound coming out of my throat is almost a whisper.

Wester leaps onto the children, pulling two back by

their arms and swearing furiously. He gives his own brat a swat, but the boy keeps lashing out wildly with his feet.

The dog is trying to escape, but every time it either falls over, or gets a boot, or rolls yelping through the dust. Carla screams at the dog. Amanda, Lily, half the village is all worked up and trying to grab a child. The Meerten boy runs off crying. Wester's kid trips over his bike. One moment the square is full of noise breaking over the houses like a wave, the next instant it's quiet. The water rolls back. A few children stand around looking dazed, others are sobbing against a wall or their mother's legs. The adults look at each other panting. Silence.

"You said yourself you felt like kicking their heads in," Wester's son whimpers in his father's arms. With his head turned away, he points back at the square, at the dog, which happens to still be there.

All eyes turn to the limping animal. It disappears around the corner with its tail between its legs, heading up the path to Helen's.

"Here, you miserable creature!" shouts someone behind the houses.

I recognize Helen's voice. She swears without swear words. No other woman knows so many ways to make a Belgian sheep dog slink and quiver. I hope she doesn't notice the stiff leg. I hope she doesn't come here.

"Move, bitch!"

The dog yelps.

I take a couple of steps toward the path, but that's as far as I get because Carla has grabbed me roughly by one arm.

"Don't you dare, Dantine!" She makes my name sound rough and common and gives me a shove, so hard that I have to take a step back to keep my balance. "Things are bad enough already. Don't make them worse. Children come up with the weirdest games. This has nothing to do with us."

Carla keeps one eye on the path, jumpy because Helen could come around the corner, scared that I might run off anyway and tell Helen what's happened.

But I'm in no hurry. What difference does it make whether I go to Helen now or later? I bat away Carla's hand. Fine, I think, I've got plenty of time, and I give her a dirty look. The blush on her face disgusts me, and those drooping, lying eyes of hers are even worse.

She herds me along in front of her—I can smell her sour sweat—and tells me that I have to help Walda and the children. That I have to help gather wood for the bonfire. She'll finish my bit of the tent.

"Hop to it, girl, Walda's already ..."

I tap her shoulder sharply.

"Don't go giving me orders," I say, "I'm not my mother. And you're not my mother." I hold my breath and turn on my heels. She's not worth another word. Very slowly, just to annoy her, I stroll past the tent, headed for the road to Volcker Wood.

"You've still got some growing to do."

When I was five I could count the kids from the valley on the fingers of one hand: Bock's daughter, who spent more time at boarding school than she did at home and didn't come home later, either; Amanda's son, an overgrown pimple who would later do an apprenticeship at a butcher's; and beyond that, Walda and me. There were others, but they lived near the expressway and liked to form gangs of their own. They never played with the kids from the valley.

I looked up to Walda. I called her my best friend. In the morning she took me to kindergarten, and in the afternoon she walked home with me. She got to go to school on the bus, because she went to big kids' school. She knew lots. One of the things she knew and liked to tell was the story of how I was born, and how I wouldn't have been here if she hadn't been there.

I admired her for her big mouth. She wasn't afraid of telling off the sons of Bruwaen the dairyman, and she dared to swear at the top of her voice on the steps of the church. If we got into a fight with an expressway gang, she would kick and lash out, then shoot off like a rocket, swearing, with me giggling along behind.

Walda's mother reinforced our friendship. I always felt nervous around Carla. She said what she thought, and that was something my beautiful mother never did. Carla was so noisy that I was a little scared of her, but I never let it show. She was too good at baking waffles. She set up the ironing board as an extra table and turned her kitchen into a stall, and with night falling and the whole house smelling of waffles, she would stuff me full and let me mess around with molasses and powdered sugar the way she'd messed around with flour and batter. When I was eating waffles, I called Walda my best friend.

But I wasn't her best friend. A few days before my seventh birthday, she let me know that she only hung out with me by lack of choice—there was nothing better available.

We were at our regular after-school hangout: up on the hill, near the birch that grows so crooked you can sit on its trunk. Before us lay pastures of clover and a gently sloping cornfield. The ears were ripe for harvest and the stalks were like bamboo. The whole field was one big rustling blanket and the wind was shaking it out. In the distance, the sky was orange above Volcker Wood. A thin ribbon of cloud was drifting over the trees.

Walda hummed like a diesel and held onto an imaginary steering wheel. She bounced up and down and swayed back and forth, as if we were driving on a dirt road, and I copied her, without taking my eyes off the clouds. They weren't sheep clouds or fluff you could see faces in.

"Where are they going?" I asked, pointing.

Walda was still playing her game. I could tell from her voice.

"They're not going anywhere," she said. "They're coming from somewhere. They come out of a great big chimney. Click." She pretended to open the car door. "I'm going to do the shopping. You wait in the car. Clunk!"

I watched her walk away. She went into the bushes to pick some leaves. When she came back she would say that they were meat and bread.

The clouds were more interesting. The whole sky was more interesting. I thought about my father and my mother. The time they stood in our backyard looking out over the fields with their arms around each other. My father said something about the sky and the earth and how they were always together. And then he kissed my mother.

Walda's voice made me jump.

"Click. You're glad to see me again and you ask me what I got. Clunk."

"What did you get?" I said, still thinking about my father and my mother.

Walda started the car. "Meat and bread," she said, and she bounced up and down and swayed back and forth.

I forgot that we were driving. Without taking my eyes off the sky, I slid down the trunk. I heard Walda say, "Outta the way, outta the way," but the words didn't get through to me.

"The sky and the earth," I whispered. "The earth and the sky."

Walda's hands dropped to her lap.

"What?" she said.

"The sky and the earth," I said. "They're always together. *Kissss*."

It was quiet. Walda stared at me. She opened her mouth, but it took a while for sound to come out of it.

"*Kissss*," she said. "That word's a size too large for you."

I thought she meant that my mouth was too small for all those s's.

"My mouth is big enough," I said.

"Maybe, but you've still got some growing to do," said Walda, pulling her sweater down tight over the bumps she had.

"You've got some growing to do, too," I said.

Walda coughed. "Not that much," she said.

I sat down next to her again. I couldn't have cared less about the car. The only thing that mattered to me now was the sky and the earth and *kissss*.

"It's funny," I said.

"What's funny?" asked Walda, who was trying to look down at her chest.

"Kissing and that," I said.

Walda didn't react.

"If I just knew," I said.

"What? If you just knew what?"

"How and everything."

Walda gave an exasperated sigh, took me by the arm, and pulled me up close. She grabbed me by the chin. "You press your mouth up against mine, it's that simple," she said.

I blinked. Before I had a chance to get ready, she cupped a hand around the back of my neck and pressed her wet lips up against mine. I pushed her away.

Walda nodded. "That is kissing," she said, and then, as if nothing had happened, she stuck her arms back out in front of her and gripped her wheel.

I sat there staring like a rag doll. Was that it? Was that all? Daddy's voice sounded a lot softer when he said that about the sky and the earth. His voice was like tissue paper rustling in his throat. It didn't go with something as hard and wet as Walda's lips.

She'd parked the car. I only noticed after things had been quiet for a while. Walda was thinking. She stared vacantly at the distant wood, or maybe even over the tops of the trees, and I felt worried and looked out with her, at the cornfield, at the forest, over the tops of the trees.

"Actually," said Walda suddenly, "actually, there is another kind of kiss. One that's harder. I think." She frowned. "I'm not sure, I saw it in a movie once." She looked at me darkly and said, "Open your mouth." She turned and straddled the trunk. "I said, open your mouth."

I thought she wanted to play doctor. Walda was the boss. She was the oldest. And my friend.

I tried to look serious, seriously sick, and groaned, holding a hand to my head. "It hurts," I said, closing my eyes and sticking out my tongue.

"Ah," I said. "Ah!"

I waited. I was expecting a hand on my cheek. A finger under my chin.

Not a tongue in my mouth.

I opened my eyes wide, made a choking noise, and gagged, but Walda refused to take her mouth off of mine. I wriggled, I pinched, I pushed. She sucked, she glued her tongue to the roof of my mouth, it felt like she'd never come loose again. I thought about what you do to meat in your mouth. I thought about biting.

Then I did what I was thinking: I bit.

Walda jumped up. She sucked in her cheeks, wiped some blood off her lips, looked at her hand, and slapped me, sending me flying backward off the tree with my legs in the air.

"You blat," she screeched. "You 'tupid blat!"

FOUR

Walda looks up, moving her weight onto her left foot and rocking her hips.

"Are you coming or not?"

I shake my head and watch the cheering children run into Volcker Wood. Their voices linger under the tall trees. There's nothing half-hearted about that sound: they won't come back until they've found every bit of dead wood in the whole forest.

"No," I say. "I don't mind looking for wood, but not here."

"Grow up."

"No," I say. "I don't mind helping, but not in this forest."

"Fine." She brushes a lock of hair out of her face. "Stay a kid." She sniffs—showing clearly that she herself is elevated above all kids—and walks over to the tall gate at the forest entrance. The gate is locked with a heavy double chain wrapped loosely around the bars.

Walda wriggles through the opening, which leaves a smudge of rust on the side of her jeans. She's about to flick it off, but when she sees that I'm still staring at her coldly through the gate, her hand stays where it is, hanging in midair.

"Look, Susanna," she says. "You don't feel like talking to me. Fine by me. You don't feel like helping. That's fine as well. You're pissed off because of your mother. I can understand that. But it's no reason to play the teenage princess. That's what gets on my nerves." She bends forward, toward the gate. "You think looking for wood doesn't bore me just as much? Someone has to look after the kids. And we just happen to be it!"

We, we, I repeat inside my head. You said yourself that you should use the word "I" if you're by yourself.

"You just happen to be it," I say. "You're not getting me into that forest."

Walda looks over her shoulder down the lane—where the kids seem to be doing fine without any babysitting—purses her lips, and strides off. Patches of sunlight glide over her back.

Later, back in the village, she'll tell anyone who cares to listen that I'm pig-headed and lazy-boned. Typical fourteen. I can almost hear her testing out the sound of it already.

I chew on my lip and think it over while I watch the children dragging dry branches into the lane. No, I'm not going into that forest, I repeat to myself in hundreds of variations. No, I am not going into that forest. But where should I go then? I look left and right down the path. There's no wood here. There's nothing but knee-high grass and a wall of corn. No dead wood. The forest is the only place you find dead wood. Nowhere else.

I turn around to face the gate. Walda's comments have set me to doubting. Into the forest to keep the peace? Into the forest because there's enough gossip about the Dantines already? I go down on my knees. Literally. I push the gate open as far as it will go and wriggle through the gap on all fours. I smell the crushed grass and the forest floor. For a second, I stay sitting. I can still turn back. I can go back to the path. I can take any direction I like.

It's only when I'm standing on the other side of the gate that I realize I've forgotten to be true to myself. I've always sworn that I would never set foot in Volcker Wood again. My throat is dry, as if I've gone weeks without water.

I walk down the lane, and instead of numbers, I count my steps with "Sorry, Daddy! Sorry, Daddy! Sorry, Daddy!"

Walda grins at me from between the ferns.

"Susanna?" she calls. "Could you please see what's keeping the little Wester kid? He went that way!" She points in the direction of the summerhouse, at least twenty Sorry, Daddies down the track.

I do what she asks, without thinking. Now that I'm here, I might just as well see if the summerhouse is still standing. There's hardly anything left of the path that leads to it. The farther I go—Sorry, Daddy! Sorry, Daddy!—the more I'm closed in by ferns. Near the summerhouse, the slate cupola rises above the undergrowth, and I have to step high to force my way through the ferns.

The lane through the forest disappears, the children's voices get fuzzy.

"The whole tree!" is the last thing I hear.

A shriek sends a shiver down my spine, but it's only a pheasant off on the edge of the forest. In front of me, behind the light and dark green foliage, I catch a flash of bright red. Since I'm not fourteen all the time, but sometimes a little girl of seven who sees old stories in rustling bushes, I freeze.

"Hey!"

No answer.

"Hey!" I say, even louder.

The rustling stops. The Wester kid feels trapped, of course.

Treading firmly, I plow through the ferns. I'm planning on taking some of my anger out on others. The brat has it coming anyway, because of the dog.

I push a rhododendron branch aside and stand there as if I've come to a dead-end. My eyes shoot from left to right, from the boy to the puppeteer. They're sitting opposite each other in the summerhouse, and both of them look up at me.

"Hey," says the puppeteer.

"Susanna!" says the Wester kid with a big grin. "Wolf is teaching me how to do it."

"How to do what?"

"The puppets," he says, lifting up the two marionettes. "I'm teaching them to dance."

"Dancing is a slight exaggeration," says the puppeteer,

giving me a wink. "He has enough trouble just holding them."

He's sitting there like a young father. Everything about him merging in that warm, gentle voice. If only someone could touch you with a warm, gentle voice like that.

I feel the blood rising to my cheeks. I tell myself that my heart is pounding with fury, but the words I squeeze out of my throat sound sweet, not even annoyed, "You're here to look for wood, not play with puppets."

"No, not play with puppets," echoes the puppeteer.

"He has to look for wood for the bonfire," I say, but it still comes out sweeter than I mean it to.

"Yep," nods the puppeteer, "he has to look for wood."

The Wester kid doesn't understand who's talking to who, and I'm not so sure myself, either.

The puppeteer's smile is confusing me. He has a gorgeous mouth, and it's laughing at me—I think.

"You," I say as angrily as I can, pointing at the boy, "did you hear what I just said? Walda's looking for you. She wants to know what's keeping you and your wood."

"But ..."

"No buts. If you promise something, you have to do it."

I sound just like folk-dancing Lily and expect another echo from the puppeteer, but none comes. There are only distant voices in the woods.

"Well?" This time the threat comes of its own accord. That kid's getting on my nerves. If he doesn't get a move on, he'll get the slap I've been saving up all afternoon.

"Did you hear me?" I say. "Go and ..."

"Look for wood," says the puppeteer. He puts the marionette with the red dress on his knee and moves its arms.

The child's face clears. Apparently, he's less obstinate with puppets. Or is he less obstinate with the puppeteer?

"Wolf wants you to," says the Spanish dancer, pointing at the puppeteer. "And that girl wants you to," the marionette points at me. "And I want you to. I'll teach you how to dance next time. That's a promise."

The Wester kid even nods his head.

How does the puppeteer do it?

The child says, "Bye!" and takes off. He comes back to pick up a dry branch, then disappears again behind the rhododendrons. He's already calling out to Walda that he made the puppets dance, and that he's got a new friend who's already grown up, but still plays with puppets.

I chuckle and look at him.

"You handled that well."

"Better than you," he answers, letting the Spanish lady droop.

What's he mean, better than me? His pretty mouth just keeps on smiling, and his eyes aren't giving anything away, either.

"You should go now," I say. "Soon you'll have a whole bunch of kids on top of you. I don't know if you'll handle them so well then." I'm shocked by the sharpness of my own tongue, and so is he. But the next instant he's recovered his smile. Broader than ever, as if he likes it when people talk back.

He jumps up, brushes the moss off his jeans, and grabs his bag. Carefully, almost tenderly, he folds up the marionette. He arranges the ribbon on her dress and smoothes her hair, and seems to have forgotten I'm even there.

I think, I can go now. I don't have to say good-bye. I don't even know his name. Or do I?

"You're called ... er ... Wolf?"

He looks up and nods.

"Wolf?"

"Yeah." He nods again. "Short for Wolfgang."

"Oh. I see. Wolf. This is a forest."

He sniggers once, smiles with that pretty mouth of his, and looks up at the treetops. I see him thinking, so, a forest, is it?

"Forget it," I say hurriedly. "Forests, fairy tales, wolves, you know." I wave my hands and feel like I should have left already.

Children's voices are approaching from behind the bushes, and the bushes seem to be closing in on me, too.

"Here they come," I say. I turn around and bend over to duck under a low-hanging rhododendron branch on my way to the edge of the forest. Walda can look after the kids. There are too many memories in Volcker Wood. Under the rhododendron is the quickest way out.

"Wait for me," says the puppeteer. He throws his bag over his shoulder and dives into the bushes behind me.

The branch I let go of swishes past his face.

Kicking my way through the ferns, I reach the edge of the forest. Light and air.

I jump over the narrow stream and the puppeteer jumps with me.

It's only now that I feel like I can breathe again and see color. My blood is flowing again. With my hands on my knees, I catch my breath. Thinking, what have we got to say to each other? How can I make him smile at me again?

"And you?" he says suddenly.

"What about me?"

"Are you really called ... er ... Susanna?" He's quiet, as if tasting my name on his lips.

The voices of excited children reach us through the trees. I make out the words "here a minute ago."

"Are you really called Susanna?" Wolf asks again. "Susanna like the chaste girl in the Bible story?"

It's only when I'm sure that his pretty mouth isn't laughing at me that I dare to nod. To snicker.

"That's right," I say.

He smiles. I did it. I made him smile at me again. I blush a bright red. My blood isn't flowing anymore, it's steaming.

"Bye," I blurt out, already walking away. He sees that I'm leaving, takes a few steps toward me, and stops me with a question, "Hey, hey, do you come here often?"

"Why, do you?" I say—ridiculously.

"I do. Don't you?"

"No, never. I ..." I grin and keep on grinning. In a

minute my cheeks will split open.

"At least it's quiet in a forest," he says, staring at the treetops. Another smile is gliding over his lips. I'd like to frame him and take him home. "Except today it wasn't so quiet," he says. "I almost jumped out of my skin when that little kid popped up out of nowhere."

"I can imagine," I say, incapable as I am of thinking of anything more sensible.

"Don't you like quiet?" he asks.

What's that got to do with anything? I think, but I say, "No, I do. I like everything that, er ... My father was ..."

"Go on," says Wolf.

A vet, I want to say, but I interrupt myself. I shake my head, shrug my shoulders, and say, "Just because."

"A surprise."

Because of this. On my seventh birthday, seven
hunters, seven dogs, fourteen beaters, and a mistress of
hounds—the only woman in the company—arrived at
Volcker's estate.

The beaters were local farmers hired for the occa-
sion. They had to spend the whole day shouting and
hitting the bushes with sticks to chase pheasant, hare,
and rabbit out of the forest. The mistress of hounds, the
gamekeeper's wife, looked after the hunting dogs and
collected the kill on a wheelbarrow. The seven
hunters—or were there more?—didn't even need to get
their hands dirty. The men—respected gentlemen one
and all—simply took position on the edge of a field facing the forest and waited for the game to appear. They
then fired, with light-gauge or heavy-gauge shot, de-
pending on the range and the kind of animal they were
after. Afterward, they strolled to the next field and the
next stretch of forest, ready for new surprises to pop up.

Like every year, Volcker was opening the hunting season with a drive in the forest. The squire had a heart, it was true, but it was an old heart with little respect for animals, even though he opened his hunt on the day before Animal Day. The story about Volcker went that he thought today's young men were lily-livered and weak-kneed because they denied their hunting instinct.

My father knew what Volcker's hunts were like. The family had invited him once, before I was born. My father had stuck to his principles and refused to carry a gun, but it was important for a vet with a new practice to be friendly and win over his fellow villagers. And Volcker.

On my birthday I woke up early. It was still dark outside. I pricked up my ears and tried to hear a dog barking or a puppy whimpering, but it was quiet in the house. Maybe I'd get a rabbit as a present. You can't hear rabbits. I was sure of it: this time my present would have ears and paws and lungs, and I'd squeeze it so tight I'd take its breath away. I think I was needing a hug myself right then.

I hadn't said a word about Walda's tongue. Not to my father, not to my mother, and not to Helen, either, even though I'd spent all of yesterday afternoon at her place.

I sat through a disappointing breakfast without any sign of an animal. There were seven candles on a cinnamon loaf, and the whole kitchen smelled like it was made of chocolate, but I had to wait for my birthday present.

"Did you see them?" my mother asked my father.

"Who?"

"Volcker and his men. Hunting. Soon the bullets will be whistling around our ears again."

"Hmmm," said my father sleepily, buttering my bread.

For a second my mother looked at me cheerily, but she soon turned back to my father with a worried expression on her face.

"Do we really need to go out for a walk? You're not serious, are you? With those hunters everywhere."

"Don't exaggerate so much, Edith. We'll check where the hunters are first."

"Hmmm," went my mother.

After breakfast they sent me out into the garden. You only had to jump over the low brick wall and you were in the fields. It was like the whole world was our backyard. Sow thistles grew between the wall and the field. Tall prickly plants that still had some yellow flowers on them. My room outside was in between the green leaves. I raked grass up into a pillow, brought out my usual pile of books, sketch pad, and colored pencils, and spent the whole morning there by myself. I didn't need Walda.

I drew the early fall of that year. A sun over a green landscape, with here and there a few licks of yellow, a few licks of brown. Two horses—a mare and a foal—in a field. A funny-looking rabbit called Walda.

Suddenly my father was standing on the wall above me.

"Suzie?"

I looked up in fright.

"What are you doing here by yourself? Why aren't you playing with Walda?"

He hunched down beside me and laid his big hands

on my shoulders. He didn't say anything else, and waited for my answer.

I didn't have an answer. More exactly: I didn't want to give one. I looked at the drawing on my knees and tried not to think about Walda. Listen to the tractor on the farm, I told myself, listen to the sparrows having an argument.

An argument.

"I ..." I couldn't finish. "Walda ..." I started again. "Sh ... no, we ..." I couldn't put it into words. I wasn't able to make sentences that went any further than subjects.

Gently my father pulled me toward him and turned my head until I was facing him.

"Walda's mother was just here," he said. "Is it true what she says? Did you really bite Walda?"

I wanted to deny it, but there was no point. Daddy could tell by looking at me that it was true. Before he had time to get angry, I got angry first. That was the smartest thing to do.

"It really hurt her bad," I said. "With her tongue and and and ..." I gasped for breath and searched for something to distract my father. "And I want a pet for my birthday!"

"Do you now?" sang my father, holding me back a little so that he could see what I was angriest about. He fell for it. He always fell for it. His eyes were shining now, so he couldn't be mad anymore.

"You'll get your pet soon enough," he said.

He smiled at the face I made.

"One of these days," he said. "An animal to look after.

A friend. We'll see about today. We'll have some cake soon, and there'll be a piece for Walda as well. And afterward we're going for a long walk. And afterward, after that, Mommy and I have a surprise for you!"

"A pet," I whispered.

"A surprise," said my father.

I nodded enthusiastically.

"Promise me you'll never bite Walda again?"

I had to think about that. I didn't want to see Walda ever again.

Daddy sighed and stroked my cheek. "Don't look so angry," he said. "Shall we finish your drawing? How can we make that animal look a bit friendlier?"

"With spit," he answered himself, "with magic pencil and some spit." He pulled me onto his lap and painted a happy red rabbit with watercolor pencil and spit.

After lunch we walked to Volcker Wood. My mother was right: close by and in the distance, gunshots echoed like hammers on nails. But in the sunken lane it was quiet, except for a woodpecker impersonating a machine gun. Now and then a pheasant shrieked in the bushes, as if it was being shot to shreds.

"Volcker must be starting this year with a field hunt after all," said my father.

I skipped along in front of my parents.

My father took photos that would later end up in our album. Alongside my funny rabbit.

Susanna, seven years old.

He took a photo of me between the rows of beeches.

Sunbeams fell through the leaves and my hair was golden.

"Watch the birdie!" called my mother, and I looked up at the highest branches of the trees. It made a really beautiful photo.

Susanna looking for the birdie.

My beautiful mother didn't stop smiling, and whenever she got a chance she held hands with my handsome father. Sometimes she grabbed him for a three-minute kiss, and then I'd stop skipping to watch how they did it.

One time I shouted out that it was my birthday and that I was supposed to get the hugs, and then my father stormed up to me, turned me over with my head in the leaves, and shouted, "No hugs for you!"

I roared with laughter, planted my hands on the ground, and stayed there with my legs sticking up. I was so surprised I forgot to laugh.

"Don't move!" Daddy shouted, and, letting go of me carefully, he began walking backward with one finger in the air. He took two photos.

Susanna, upside down.

I fell over and stayed sitting in the leaves. I saw my father looking back proudly at my mother.

"I stood on my head!" I called out. It turned into a song inside my head, and a song out loud, and I walked along behind my parents singing it, going down the path to the summerhouse.

"If by Michaelmas the acorns lie, the winter winds will howl and cry," said my mother. "Maybe it'll be a cold ..."

Noise shredded the forest silence. Shots sounded everywhere, in the distance and close by. We could hear the beaters yelling and hitting bushes with their sticks. The trees held their breath. Nothing moved.

"We're going back," said my mother.

The racket of gunshots died down.

"Before the beaters get here"—my father was silent for a moment, because the guns had fallen silent as well—"we'll be home long before they get here, sweetheart. We'll go back in a minute." He sounded calm and sure of himself. I dared to let go of my mother.

The woodpecker went back to its impersonation. The pheasants didn't seem to be screaming as loudly as before, either.

"Don't look so angry," my father told my mother. He gave her a kiss, turned to me, and said, "What do you think, Suzie? A game of hide-and-seek?"

No sooner had I nodded than my father was off like a flash, down the path and across the lane.

I saw him disappear into the rhododendrons, covered my face with my hands, and started counting. From one to ten, and then ten times.

My mother helped me. She held my face pressed up against her stomach. "No peeking," she said.

After ten times I called out loudly, "Coming ready or not!"

The very same instant, a volley of shots rang out. My mother jumped. Maybe my father did, too.

The story about Volcker went that he had never shot a fellow before.

FIVE

"Oh," says Wolfgang.

"That's why," I say.

I lie down on my back in the grass, suddenly exhausted. The treetops above me are hardly moving, the sky is low. I close my eyes. I see green and yellow spots.

"That's terrible," Wolf says from somewhere far away. "Just terrible. I'm sorry but ... He promises you a surprise for your birthday and then you get—pardon the expression—a surprise like that."

I nod without opening my eyes and pretend that after all this time the remark doesn't shock me anymore. I realized what a cruel joke it was years ago. It doesn't shock me anymore, it only makes me shrink a little, somewhere far away and faint and deep inside me.

My birthday surprise was a dog. I know that from my mother. A pup from the kennel. There was a fresh litter of seven, but I never went to pick out the most beautiful. The animal would have grown big on memories. Its every whimper would have made my beautiful mother and me think of the old days. For years to come it would have reminded us of my father, even when it wagged its tail.

"Was it very long ago?" asks Wolf.

"Almost seven years," I say. My voice sounds matter-of-fact, and I'm glad of that.

"Incredible," I hear him say. "Seven years and still talking about it."

My eyes flash open. I scrunch up my eyebrows against the light, feel my mouth falling open, and hear myself hissing indignantly.

"You're the one who asked about it," I say. "How come? Tell me? Why?"

"Why?" he says. "No!" He slaps his forehead. "I mean, that they're still fighting about it here in the village."

"About what?"

"The dogs, those dogs. What's-his-name ... Volcker's dogs."

I prop myself up on one elbow, feeling a little dizzy. I have to think it through three times before I work out what he's saying. Think it through three times before I can say something back.

"Volcker? The Volckers left ages ago. Their house has been empty for three years. That fight on the square was about some other dogs."

Wolf raises his eyebrows.

"What dogs? What's up with these other dogs?"

"It's an old story," I say, lying down on my back again and sliding my hands in under my head. I purse my lips, trying to straighten out my feelings first. A whole lacework of thoughts has been growing in my mind. "Want a good laugh?"

His chin goes up, and he pulls out his pretty smile again. His lips are glistening.

"Do you really, really, really want to know?" I say, hoping he'll keep on smiling.

"Of course. I couldn't ask earlier. I'd love, love, love to know."

"Why?"

"Because ... just because." He lies on his side and re-laxes as if he's getting ready for a long story.

I hesitate. Lying there like that, he makes me think of skin. Of bare skin under his clothes. I reach out and touch him, but fortunately he can't tell by looking at me, and he can't feel it, either, because I only touch him inside my head. I cover my face with my hands, curl my fingers into fists.

"Okay. I'll keep it short," I say. "There are three sides. Helen is one. Her husband has a kennel on the other side of the village. It used to be a kennel, now it's a dog factory." I look quickly to see if Wolf is listening. He is.

"That woman on the balcony, who's she?"

"Carla. Carla is two. Last month she started a peti-tion. She said the dogs are too noisy and have to go. More or less everyone has gone along with it, just about everyone signed the petition. Except for me and my mother."

"The Heroines."

"Yes," I say in an attempt to end my story.

"And?" says Wolf.

That's all. To be continued. I can't bring myself to

talk about my mother's about-face. No, I say to myself, first a happy story about how much fun everything was in the old days.

Slowly I shake my head.

"What do you mean, no? Your mother can handle that woman Carla, can't she?"

"She could," I sigh, brushing aside Wolf's questions. "I don't feel like explaining. I have to go anyway, they're waiting for me."

I get up and avoid Wolf's eyes, hoping that he'll try to stop me, that he'll say we can talk about something else, about the weather, about music, about the city, but at the same time I realize that he probably thinks I'm a country bumpkin, a chaste girl from the Bible, someone who couldn't even hold up her end of a conversation about skipping rope. How could he think of me as anything but a country bumpkin, after all those small-time stories of mine. Forget about him, I think. Just forget about it. The less you know about him, the easier he'll be to forget.

"Bye. See you around maybe," I say.

"Stay here," he says, but I've made up my mind. His eyes burn into my back as I scramble up. For God's sake, I say to myself. What are you doing, Susanna? What are you? Some kind of pigeon that can't wait to fly home?

His scooter is half-hidden in the bushes at the end of the path. What happened to my secret fantasy? Racing at high speed through the streets, up and down the hill?

I walk past the gate, Walda could appear any moment. One ear is listening for screaming children, the other hears footsteps. My heart skips a beat.

Wolf takes me by surprise.

"Come on!" He retraces his footsteps, wheels the scooter out from between the bushes, straps his bag on the back, and straddles the seat. He revs up the engine.

"Come on!" he shouts above the racket. His pretty mouth isn't laughing now. His eyes are asking for a smile from me, I think. His whole body is telling me it's strong enough for two.

Come on, pigeon, flashes through my mind, and I climb onto the back, place my hands cautiously on his hips, and tighten my grip when the scooter takes off with a jolt and shoots out onto the path. I'm so thrilled I can hardly breathe.

There's no wind, just warm air gliding past. Every bump sends me flying. What am I supposed to do with my hands? The seat is smooth with nowhere to hold on. And everything above it is his.

"Yes!" he yells suddenly. And again, "Yes."

I laugh in nervous little bursts. Do all his girlfriends giggle this loud? Do all his girls breathe in as deeply as they can, just to get a little bit of his air in their lungs?

Over his shoulder I see the village square coming closer. Almost too late I realize that I can't arrive at the square like this. In a panic, I tug at his shirt.

He brakes abruptly, sending me bumping forward with my cheek against his back. I jump off. A few houses farther, just around the corner, is the tent, and I don't want anyone seeing me. Not with him. The next thing I know it will be on Amanda's front page.

"Bye," I say quickly, but he stops me.

"What about me?" he asks, nodding at the square.

"There's a party on," I say.

"For me, too?" he says.

"For everyone," I say.

"Ah," he says.

He revs the engine of his scooter, makes a U-turn, and races off.

"Say 'Bye-bye, Daddy.'"

After Father Drecht left, my mother told me to put away my building blocks and asked me if I wanted to see Daddy. She took me to the bedroom door, hesitated, then pushed me along in front of her, up the three steps.

Two candles at the foot of the bed flickered in the draft. The flames cast shadows on the walls.

I stood close to my mother and held my breath. I had never seen my mother this quiet before. Her eyes were puffy and red around the lashes. It's more than just a cold, I thought.

My father was in the big bed. In the middle, where I always lay when my father and mother let me creep in between them on Sunday mornings. His hands were together and his hair was neatly combed.

"Daddy isn't sleeping," said my mother out of nowhere.

She pulled my head up against her hip, lay a dry hand on my cheek, and kept on stroking me with one finger.

I got a queasy feeling in my tummy and my throat swelled up. I hadn't understood what had gone wrong with my father, but now, with my mother keeping quiet for so long and the silence weighing so heavy, I suddenly figured it out.

My father should have jumped up ages ago or burst out laughing or done something. A black curtain was hanging on the wall at the end of the bed where there was usually a picture of a lady without any clothes on. Instead of the painting there was a cross, a big one like they have in church. The word "dead" crept through my brain, but I was too scared to use it.

I waited for an answer and looked up at my mother, but I hadn't asked the question out loud. She stared back with eyes that looked right through me.

Slowly, I walked over to the bed and lay a hand on the velvet bedspread, close to my father's praying hands. I wanted to touch them. I hadn't thought that his hands could ever be this cold, this white, this hard.

My mother came over beside me, pulled me away from the bed, and started to cry.

I didn't understand what had happened. Why did I have to go away? Was Daddy going away? How? And where?

"Say 'Bye-bye, Daddy,'" my mother said quickly, as if they were words she couldn't wait to forget.

I lifted up a hand, but didn't have the strength to wave. The candles did that for me, when we shut the door on my father.

SIX

On the square, Wester is already so drunk I can almost smell it. His face is red—not just from chugging beer, but from lugging crates over from the store as well. The tent has turned into a party tent. Lily is busy draping the square with red and white pennants. The festoons are up on the lampposts. Tables and chairs have been set up around where the bonfire is going to be. Bunches of dried wildflowers in yogurt pots decorate the tables.

Inside the tent, the women are waxing the dance floor. Skating circles in the shade with rags on their feet. They're not worried about the heat, they're not paying any attention to the music man. Even when he turns the volume right up and the bass makes the whole square throb, they still keep on skating and chattering. Someone laughs. Not because someone else told a joke, but because they just felt like laughing.

At our place, the shutters are closed. I know that my mother is skulking behind them. She can hear what's happening outside. I hope it's annoying her. That she doesn't have the peace of mind to read one of her romantic novels. I hope she's lying on her bed with an ice pack on her head, groaning from a headache like she always does.

I zigzag past the tables, heading for the uphill path at the back of the houses. I'm breathless from the scooter ride, my legs are still shaky from the motor. I look down at the ground, as if that makes me less conspicuous, but no one's paying any attention. If they were, Carla would have called out ages ago. After all, I'm going in a direction she doesn't like.

A blackbird hops along in front of me. He lets his wings droop, drowsy from the heat shimmering above the valley. The roadside crickets are chirping louder than normal, it sounds like they're screaming.

The orchard in front of Helen's house is peaceful. That won't last long. In a minute, when I come around the bend and take the road that leads through the apple trees to the kennel, the quiet will be over. I can already hear the racket the dogs will make. The barking, howling, growling, whining.

I hesitate and stop where I am, just before the curve. I can hear someone humming, but there's no one on the road in front of me or behind me. I look through under the low apple trees. Farther along, I spot a pair of boots with a piece of bright apron above them.

Helen.

My heart starts to pound, my ears are ready for the

worst. I walk up the road.

At that moment, Helen turns. She sees my astonished face. My dumbfounded face. The dogs don't start up. They don't. Not at all. The valley stays quiet, except for Helen's laugh.

"The heat, Susanna!" she says. "They're sweating like pigs!" She steps over the gutter that separates the orchard from the road, lays her hands on my shoulders, and shakes me gently.

"The dogs!" I say.

"But I told you? The heat's got to them. If you listen closely, you can hear them panting from here." Helen breathes in and out heavily and pulls me along by the arm. She says she's already had some coffee, but she wouldn't mind some more.

"Don't you have to help in the tent?"

"Already have. Nobody ..."

"Listen. Listen to the silence," says Helen. She leads the way between the cages, looking right and left contentedly.

"One got away again this afternoon," she says.

"Did it?" I say.

From here and there comes a quiet growling, or a lazy bark that sounds more like an old man coughing. Most of the dogs don't even get up. A few follow us for a step or two inside their cages, but then they give up as well. On cooler days it's different. Then they bark, they growl, they make sure you know that they have only one real master, that big man with those big hands, they'd follow him blindly, and that woman in that apron of hers, they'll let her come close as well, because she's the one who feeds them.

I can't believe my ears. It's never been like this. Helen can shout, she can laugh—the dogs don't do a thing. She slams the doors in the house and sings "coffee, coffee, coffee!" and still the dogs don't bark anything back.

"I'll just be a second," she says, and disappears into the kitchen.

I listen to the familiar ticking of the living room clock, I listen to the faucet dripping in the pantry—the second ticking clock.

To get over my surprise, I sit down on my spot by the fireplace, the inch-high step in front of the hearth, which I made my spot when I was only an inch high myself. I always used to play shop or lay out my dolls' beds on it.

I sit there looking at how nothing has changed in this house. I hear Helen shouting into the opened cupboard to ask whether I want to see the new litter, I usually want to see them, or has the heat got to me, too?

I don't answer.

"A beautiful litter though," she says, coming into the living room with a tray. She's got out her Sunday cups in my honor. She gives me a Sunday smile to go with them.

"The barrel?" She hands me the tray.

"The barrel," I say.

Helen leads the way. Leaving her boots on the doorstep and holding up her apron unnecessarily high, she tiptoes through the grass to the garden shed.

Two wooden beams are balanced on the edge of the barrel, which is in between the creepers. Many's the time Helen and I have sat here relaxing with our feet in the rainwater.

The hill is steep, and with the heat trapped between the house and the slope, it's stifling. The water in the barrel feels icy cold, so that's what I scream out as I lower my feet into it.

Helen giggles and struggles to hoist herself up onto the other beam. She's getting old.

"Ice," she says, and kicks the coldness away from her feet.

"You get used to it," I say.

You do get used to it, and it perks me up, but it doesn't chase away the crowded feeling inside my head. There are so many things in there I need to think about.

I get the coffee cups ready. My hands are shaking, the spoon tinkles against the sugar bowl.

"Are you shivering?"

"No, not really."

"What's the matter? Why are your hands shaking like that?"

"It's nothing."

"Nothing, is it?"

"Nothing special," I say.

Helen puts her cup to one side and rests her open hands in her lap.

"You can't fool me."

I shrug. I haven't thought enough yet. I don't have any words for the lacework in my head. I feel like Wolf is the only beautiful thing I can talk about without thinking first. My heart is full of him.

"And?" asks Helen.

"There was this guy in the village," I say.

"And? He was nothing special?"

"No, he was. He made these puppets dance."

"Just dance?"

"It was up to us to say what he should make them do. One of the marionettes was Spanish and the other one ..."

"Us?"

"Us." Suddenly I realize where my story is going to end. "That's um ... Amanda and Dr. Bock and ..."

Helen nods. "Just about everyone."

"Yeah, just about everyone who lives on the square. So, it was up to us to say what the two puppets should do."

"And what did everyone say?"

I shoot a glance at Helen.

"All kinds of things," I blurt.

"All kinds of things?" says Helen. She's waiting.

I gulp my coffee, giving myself time to think, time to adopt an attitude.

"That's all," I say finally, "nothing special, as you can tell."

Helen slowly shakes her head.

"Suzie," she says. "You're lying. You're lying through your teeth. What was it, another brawl? No, let me guess. There was a brawl about, er ... about four-footed animals."

I look away.

In the cages on the far side of the house, a metal

trough rattles. For a moment I think that the dogs are going to start barking, I think I can hear their panting getting louder, but all I can hear is my own breathing.

"This time it went further," I say. "It went beyond brawling."

"It can't go beyond brawling."

"Yes it can," I say. "Mom signed the petition. I can hardly believe it myself."

Helen clicks down her cup. She mumbles something. She doesn't answer right away.

"No," she says. "No, something like that's not easy to believe."

"Impossible," I say.

Helen breathes out with a sigh and lifts her feet up out of the water.

"No," she says. "Not out of the blue like that."

"I think it's been getting to her for a long time."

"Is she, um, you know... ?"

I shrug. What difference does it make how she's feeling? She's done the one thing she swore she would never do. She's done it. End of story.

"No," says Helen again.

I watch her face change as she lifts her legs over the edge of the barrel. A crease appears above her eyebrows, her mouth turns mean, as if she's clenching her jaw. She becomes tough Helen. She tugs her apron straight. She's already forgotten half the conversation, she didn't catch it, she never heard it.

"That's done my feet a world of good," she says.

"Ha ha," I say, although she didn't mean it to be funny.

"Ha ha," she says, looking at me longer than necessary. For just a moment she wants to be gentle with me, not too long—being gentle is dangerous.

"Don't worry about it too much, Susanna," she says. "Try to understand your mother."

"That's not easy," I say.

One of Helen's hands goes up in the air. "Not easy?" she says. Slowly, very slowly, she lets her hand drop, so that it finally ends up on my knee. "No, it is easy. You just have to do it. Just do it. Your mother is human, too, you know."

"And your friend," I say. "A friend wants what's best for you. You just don't do things like that."

"She's not doing it to get at me, Susanna. She's doing it to get rid of the dogs. And I couldn't care less about the dogs, you know that. Take 'em away, I'd be only too happy to unlock the cages."

"But you know that..."

"What do I know?"

"That Rudy will go looking for a scapegoat. And he never looks far. He takes a quick look around, and you're always closest."

A silence falls, telling me I'm right.

"Oh well," says Helen. "That'll be my problem. It'll be no skin off anyone else's nose." She sounds like she doesn't have a friend in the world.

"And we all live happily ever after," I say. "Don't kid me that Mom's not doing something against you by signing that petition. She knows what Rudy's like, and she still put her name on that stupid piece of paper."

Helen's grip slackens. She purses her lips and nods,

more sure of herself with every nod.

"Sure. Fine," she says quietly. "It's my problem and no one else's." She stares at me for a while, then suddenly breathes in deeply through her nose, as if waking with a start. A crease appears above her eyebrows, and she changes into the tough version of herself for good. She puts the cups on the tray and crosses the lawn with it.

Halfway, she turns.

"Try to understand your mother," she says. "You know that she still has a hard time of it without your dad. Time cures all wounds. Lucky for us, when they made time, they invented patience as well."

"You want to draw a picture?"

The fire warmed the whole room, and its glow shone on Helen's face while she gave the seventh puppy its bottle. The problem pup that couldn't keep the nipple in its mouth and kept on coughing up the milk.

The mother of the seven puppies had gone funny in the head after having them. She'd kept her litter secret, and she hadn't licked her young clean. And even worse: she'd bitten the eighth pup to death and almost eaten it up.

Helen rocked the puppy like a baby and winked at me.

I smiled back, without really thinking about what I was doing. I was sitting on my step in front of the fire and wearing my prettiest clothes. There was a black ribbon in my hair, and I had on a velvet dress with a white lace collar. My blue rabbit was lying on my knees, and I was holding it by its ears. I stared at Helen's hands.

Daddy was gone. He was lying in the big bed, but

then he disappeared. Amanda from the village store said something about God. "Your Daddy's gone to God now." Father Drecht said that God was in heaven, and that sounded a long way away. Heaven is high up, higher than the trees of Volcker Wood, a lot higher than the clouds, and Daddy was up there now.

Helen waved her hand in front of my eyes.

I jumped and stared at her fingers, and at the wedding ring that made it look like one of her fingers had a gold section in between two knuckles.

I missed Mommy, and I missed Daddy even more. If I thought about him, I saw his cold, white hands. Always those cold, white hands, never his warm arms or his gentle voice.

In the distance, the church bells rang. Slow, sad, and miserable. The world stood still. There were no tractors working the farms. Even the livestock, the poultry, and the dogs in the kennels seemed to be keeping quiet.

Helen coughed and clasped her hands together.

"Would you like to look at the puppy some more?" she asked after a long silence.

I shook my head and hugged my rabbit tighter. No.

"Then I'll take him back to his brothers and sisters. Would you like some milk? Or a candy sprinkle sandwich?"

No, not now.

"I want to draw a picture," I said.

"You want to draw a picture?" Helen seemed glad that I'd finally said something, and that she was able to repeat it.

She disappeared outside with the puppy, and when

she came back she went looking for paper and pencils. She opened and closed cupboards, and slid drawers in and out, but couldn't find any stuff for drawing. Then she got a stack of paper and the stub of a pencil from Rudy's office and lay them in my lap. "Helen can't find colors," she said.

I stared at the pencil and the paper. I thought of Daddy on the brick wall, of Daddy painting my rabbit with spit.

I bent over and spat carefully on the piece of paper.

"Suzie!" said Helen, rubbing the paper dry with her hanky. "Spitting isn't drawing."

I almost spat again, but I stopped myself, because Helen didn't understand. I'd just have to draw Daddy. In ordinary gray pencil.

Helen stayed bent over for a while with her hands on her knees, looking over my shoulder.

"That's right," she said with a catch in her voice. "That's right, make a lovely drawing." And suddenly she ran into the kitchen, where she splashed water into the sink and blew her nose.

"What's with you?" sounded suddenly.

I looked toward the kitchen, but I could only hear Rudy's voice.

"Here, I got the paper. It's in it. 'By our police reporter.' I guess Volcker must have been reported to the police."

"Be quiet," said Helen.

"Ha!" said Rudy. I heard the rustle of newspaper. "Look: HUNTERS SHOOT VET."

"Put that paper away!"

Helen whispered my name, and Rudy poked his head around the side of the door. He didn't smile at me, but just disappeared again.

"I'm not staying. Make sure the dogs get fed."

The outside door closed.

I went back to my drawing. It was only after a long time that I noticed Helen standing in front of me. Her gaze slid from me to the drawing. I didn't really want to show it to her, but I did.

It was Daddy. Daddy with a gray sweater and gray pants and gray hair. All gray. Like ash.

That Thursday it got later and later, it was already dark, and my mother just didn't come to pick me up.

I'd been waiting for her on the stool next to the front door since seven o'clock. I had my tight-fitting jacket on, my suitcase was ready for departure, and I was singing quietly to myself to pass the time.

As much as I liked the clicking of Helen's knitting needles, I still couldn't wait to get home. At Helen's it was always dark, at night and in the daytime.

When the telephone rang I jumped up, but sat down again right away. The doorbell sounded different, of course.

Helen picked up the receiver, said her name, and went silent. She looked at me, then turned away. She didn't say a thing. Just before she hung up, I heard her say, "Try to rest, take a sleeping pill." She drummed her fingers on the cupboard and came over to me.

"You're staying with Helen," she said, as if she was talking about a strange lady I didn't know.

"I know, and then Mommy's coming," I said.

"No," said Helen. "Yes, that's right. You have to sleep one more night at Helen's, and then Mommy's coming."

"That was yesterday!" I said. I gestured that things that were over never came back.

Helen wrung her hands. She bent over toward me and shook her head.

"Mommy's not feeling very well, Susanna. She's sad, very sad."

Suddenly I understood what Helen meant. I had to stay another night. Here in this house where it was always dark, at night and in the daytime. I felt the corners of my mouth droop.

"Mommy's coming soon," I said, "Mommy's coming ..."

"Tomorrow," Helen nodded. She unbuttoned my jacket, peeled the sleeves off my arms, and took it and my suitcase to the room where I was going to sleep.

I wiped away my tears, clenched my fists in my skirt pockets, and decided not to move another inch. If I had to stay, I would stay right here, on my stool.

"You still here?"

Rudy was standing in the other corner of the room. I hadn't heard him come in. He was the man I'd heard lots of talk about, but had almost never heard talk. His voice was loud, so loud I could feel it in my stomach. His body filled the room, there was hardly any air left over for other people. He came out of the darkness into the circle of light under the lamp and gave a quick nod in my direction. He took off his cap.

"Hasn't she come yet?"

In one glance I saw that he still had his boots on and that they were caked with mud.

"Hey, she coming to get you or what?"

"One more night," I said.

Helen came into the room.

"Susanna's staying one more night."

"And you don't bother to ask me?"

"You know that Mr. Dantine ..." Helen opened the front door a little and sniffed up the outside air.

"Shut that door."

"It stinks here in the house. You only smell it when you come back in."

Helen picked me up and pressed her cheek against mine. "You've still got your boots on," she said casually to Rudy. She wanted to get past him, but he wouldn't get out of the way.

"I'll give her a bath, then put her to bed."

"Shut the door first."

"You shut it, you're closest. And take your boots off while you're at it."

"Tell me about it. Either you shut the door, or I'll kick it shut."

"Kick it shut then."

Helen lay a dry hand on the back of my neck, as if to protect me.

"I'll give the kid a bath and put her to bed," Rudy said, grabbing me by the arm.

"Let go of her," said Helen.

He didn't let go of me. Neither did she.

"The door, Helen. You've been messing around with

that kid all day."

"Any objections?"

"Plenty."

Helen stepped back, forcing him to let go, and his nails scraped over my arm. It didn't hurt, but, with Rudy looking at me, and Helen looking at me, and both of them with such a strange look in their eyes, my stomach flipped and turned, a lump came into my throat, and my lip trembled.

"Give the kid here and shut the door or I'll shut you up," said Rudy.

"Keep your hands off her!"

"Give her here!"

His paw again. Tugging at my arm. He had to let me go. Let me go! I started crying. Outside the dogs barked. Their barking was all through the house. Rudy screamed at Helen that she'd better let go of me now. Helen screamed at Rudy that she'd never let go. Rudy said that he'd see about that, and he tried to hit Helen, but, by accident, or maybe on purpose, his fingers hit me on the head, and I screeched and fell forward, and Helen caught me, but Rudy did the opposite of catching, he pushed us away, and Helen stumbled over the mat. I saw the room tilting, slipped out of Helen's hands, fell onto the floor, and just caught sight of Helen falling backward onto the sofa, the sofa toppling over as well, and Helen's feet shooting out from under her and her head hitting the wall.

"Rudy!" shouted my mother.

I looked up, I looked around, I must have dreamed my mother's voice, but the voice was real, my mother was really there. She was standing panting in the doorway and swearing, swearing like I'd never heard before. Rudy spun around as if he'd been stung by a bee, and scurried off into the kitchen. The outside door banged, and then we knew for sure that he was gone, and my mother started moving, and Helen scrambled up, and I threw myself blindly into my mother's arms and almost drowned in my tears. The warmth of her body, her arms, her voice—"Mommy wasn't going to bed without you!"—and my chest got all warm, and my back got nice and warm, too, because Helen was hugging my mother, and I was in a warm nest between two women, sobbing above my head for very different, but all too similar reasons.

SEVEN

Water splashes in the barrel in the garden. Inside the house, china clatters fit to shatter. And from the slope behind me comes a voice I don't want to hear.

"Helen?" The sound dies out over the valley. "Helen?" The gate behind the garden shed squeaks open.

"You there?"

My mother appears. As an apparition. She's wearing a black evening gown, a dress from the old days. Draped over her shoulders, a crocheted cardigan. She marches straight to the kitchen door. March isn't quite the right word. To my amazement, she's wearing high heels.

She stops at the door.

"Ah, there you are!" she says to the kitchen. "I wanted to ask if you were coming to the party later. And, um ... if you'd seen Susanna."

She's talking louder than usual, as if she can't hear herself properly. Inside, it stays quiet. Helen comes to the door without saying a word and points in my direction.

I change position. The water murmuring against the side of the barrel is just loud enough to make my mother look up.

Seeing me wipes the smile off her face. Her mask comes undone.

"Oh," she says. The cardigan slips off her shoulders, she bends down, picks it up.

"Pity," says Helen. "I just poured out the leftover coffee, otherwise you ..."

"Doesn't matter, we don't have time," says my mother quickly. "They're getting the barbecue ready, they've already lit the fire—as if it's not hot enough already." She laughs loudly and concentrates on her cardigan, folding it up carefully and hanging it over one arm. Her head moves in jerks. "And?" she says to Helen. "You coming down to eat sausages on the village?" Her face is hoping for a no.

"I don't think Rudy feels much like sausages on the village."

"That's a shame," says my mother. She doesn't think it's a shame, I can tell. She looks invitingly in my direction, and Walda's words flash through my mind. We, we? We is plural, I is singular. I want to be alone.

"You coming, Susanna?" I can hear the doubt in her voice. In an evening gown and with her hair up, she thinks she can maintain appearances. Snappy mother crosses lawn on high heels.

I can't look at her for too long. Looking at her for too long twists me up inside. Go away, will you? I think. Go away before Helen starts talking about the dogs. Go back to your bed and your ice pack.

"Edith?" says Helen.

My mother turns like a dancer, oh what a charming woman she is, and she sings, oh how beautifully she sings, "Mmmm, yes?"

Helen plants her hands on her hips and shakes her head. "Since when do you use the garden gate? Why did you take the long way around, over the hill?"

My mother lets out a snort of laughter. "I felt like a walk," she says.

"In those shoes?"

"Yes, in these shoes." She looks from her shoes to Helen, and then at me. I feel like either disappearing into the barrel or else walking over to my mother. Making sure she loses her balance on those high heels of hers.

"Next thing you know, you'll twist your ankle," says Helen. "Stepping in a pie up there."

My mother hesitates. So does her face. She doesn't know how she should look.

"Coming, Susanna?" she asks again.

No, I want to say.

"Yes," says Helen. "Susanna was just leaving. Weren't you, Susanna?" Again she looks at me longer than necessary, but this time the crease above her eyebrows doesn't disappear.

I can tell what she's thinking, what she's mentally ordering me to do. The dogs, think of the dogs! Today they've forgotten to bark—and your mother doesn't know!

Silently I climb out of the barrel, grab my shoes, and follow my mother into the house. As I go past, I feel Helen's warm hand in the small of my back.

"Bye," she says. Then louder, "The dogs! They need feeding. Soon they'll be whining over empty bowls." She knows how to emphasize just the right words.

My mother shrinks. Pity I can't see her face, it's too dark in the hall.

"To be honest, Helen," says my mother, "I actually came around the back because of the dogs. The noise, in the village they complain about the noise every day."

"Hmmm," says Helen, resting her hand on the doorknob. "Lately they haven't got anything to complain about." With a grand gesture she throws open the door. The sun is already low, but the light is bright enough, and my mother gasps for breath. She lifts her hands up toward the silence. For a few seconds she's flabbergasted, she forgets to say good-bye and almost stumbles down the step.

I cheer inwardly. A small triumph, but still a triumph. With every lazy growl from the dogs, I'm scared that this delicious feeling will be shattered. Quick, Mom, I think, quick. Hurry to the orchard, then it will all be behind you.

On her way into the shed where they fix the dog food, Helen waves.

I think it's fantastic, I love it. My mother's straight, tense back, the hesitant way she steps over the orchard's shadows. She doesn't look back once. When we take the road to the village, I can hear her despair in the clicking of her heels on the pavement. Until she suddenly stops and groans, as if feeling a stab of pain in her stomach. In one movement she turns and slaps me.

"How could you?" she hisses. "How dare you make a fool of your own mother? Satisfied now? Did you tell Helen everything? Well? Did you drag me through the mire? Me, your mother?"

My cheek is burning. In one shot, my mother blasts away everything I wanted to say.

"Child!" She spits the word in my face. "You're a child, and children don't get mixed up in the affairs of grown-ups. Understood?" Her eyes are dark. "Understood? I know exactly what I'm doing, even if you think otherwise. I happen to have lived a little longer than you, and more than fourteen years of that in this village. This godforsaken dump of a village." She's shaking all over, as if she's got sunstroke.

"Stop it," I say.

"You, you're the one who has to stop it!" she says. "You're my daughter and you have to do what I say! If they want to get rid of the dogs, then I want to get rid of them, too. I want some peace in my life for once!"

Her shrieking whisper gives me the creeps. It disgusts me and makes me angry all at once, and I'm scared that someone will hear her. I've never seen her like this before. I grab her by the arms, find the courage not to give her a shaking, and whisper, "Mom, stop it. Stop it. Stop it."

She presses her lips together, breaks free of me, and stops. For ages she stands there breathing heavily. She rubs her throat, runs her fingers through her hair, swallows, and swallows again.

I think about what Helen said to me about time and wounds and patience. I think about what I said about understanding. Slowly my mother calms down. I feel the fury subsiding within me, the sounds of the party on the village square get happier and happier, the sun sinks deeper and deeper, the feeding troughs rattle and—of course, the thing that always happens finally happens—the dogs start up, they bark, they whine, they whimper, the way they always do.

EIGHT

The smell of sausage and grilled tomato drifts through the closed shutters and the open window and into the bathroom. The party keeps on getting noisier, as if the music is being turned up by the minute and everyone just shouts louder to make themselves heard.

As loud as it is, my ears block it out. My head is already crowded enough with voices, it's pounding. A hundred times my mother repeats what she said this afternoon, she gives me another hundred slaps. Every time, Helen repeats that I have to try to understand my mother, and Carla never stops trying to pick a fight, and Walda laughs at me, and Wolf smiles.

He smiles. He's the only one who's quiet, wisely silent, but at the same time saying so much. He watches, and the look on his face tells me he's going to help me. He watches me in everything I think and do. I'll help you think. I'll help you.

Even when I get out of the bath and walk to my room with a towel wrapped around me and stand in front of the wardrobe mirror, he's still watching me. Oh, he says with his eyes. Oh.

I let the towel slide to the floor. If the shutters blew open now, I'd be in full view of the whole village. I stick out my chest and push back my bottom, just to give them something to look at. Oh.

I decide what to wear. I pick out something I like and my mother hates: my shortest dress. If she says a word, I'll tell her it's too hot for anything longer.

The door to my mother's bedroom squeaks open. Her heels tap down the three steps and walk straight to the front door, which closes with a click. She's not even coming to see whether I pass muster.

"Who do we have here!" I hear Carla shout.

My mother's answer gets lost in the uproar, but Carla's voice cuts through everything.

"On your lonesome?" That tone of hers. Why doesn't my mother stick up for herself?

I walk to the window and peep out through the wooden slats. Sunlight, the colors of a summer evening. No matter how much I tie myself in knots, I can't get Carla into my field of vision.

"Come on, grab a plate and eat!" she says, as if she made the sausages herself.

My mouth falls open with amazement. I discover my mother in the crowd. She's sitting over on the left, not far from our front door, and she's alone, so that's not right. Carla's voice is coming from the other side, from somewhere near the church.

I push open the shutters, flinch from the noise, and look for Carla. I scan the square from left to right, and suddenly there she is: her cheeks are glowing with the heat. She puts some tomato on a plate and hands it to a young guy standing in front of her. The young guy standing in front of her is Wolf.

I slam the shutters as if I've seen a ghost. In no time flat I've fished my shoes out from under the bed—almost putting them on the wrong feet—and combed back my hair. Racing out of my bedroom, I don't even stop to look back to see whether my underpants are showing under my skirt or whether I look pretty enough. I take a deep breath, and another, and step into the party.

"Come and sit here, look at you," says my mother from her chair. "Your ... your hair is still wet."

"It'll dry," I say, sliding onto a chair across the table from her. Ready to jump up again at any moment. As inconspicuously as I can, I let my gaze pass over the square, trying to catch sight of long black hair, a denim shirt, and jeans in between all the floral shirts and sequined skirts.

"There's no one there," my mother says. She thinks I'm checking whether I'll have to line up for the village's unrivaled sausages. "Go get a plate. Carla will throw something on it for you."

"I'm not ..."

I see Wolf's hair first. Then I see all of him. He's sitting at the top of the church steps as if he's been given a place of honor. My stomach shrinks, I definitely won't be able to swallow a mouthful now. I turn back to my mother.

She stares at me, looks at the broad smile on my lips. Her mouth, with a mush of sausage inside it, is hanging half-open. Slowly she lowers her knife and fork, chews, and swallows.

"What are you grinning at?" she asks, impaling a piece of tomato with her fork. "Seen him, have you, the hero? What's he doing here? Carla didn't waste any time buttering him up." She jams the tomato into her mouth and swallows it straight down. "You wouldn't see me coming back to a place like this."

What kind of place would you go back to? Your bed? Your kitchen behind closed shutters? Your reading corner on the sofa?

The grin is still on my lips. Nerves are jangling through my whole body, but the grin on my face is permanent.

"They can do what they like. It's their party, not mine," mumbles my mother with her eyes on her plate.

No, it's not her party, thank God. Otherwise, we'd all be falling asleep in front of a string orchestra.

I look around quickly, to see whether Wolf is still sitting there. Amanda has gone over to him. She's shaking with laughter, her mouth opening and closing as if she's catching flies. Wolf's laughing, too, naturally, the way he always does. With those gleaming eyes and his Adam's apple dancing above his open-necked shirt.

"Ask him if he wants to marry you," says my mother suddenly. Her own remark perks her up.

The grin glides from my face after all. My mood sinks after all, especially once she's fueled the fire. "He's right there in front of the church, you can go straight in."

I slide my chair away from the table.

My mother giggles a little, then stiffens up. She thinks I really am going to go ask him.

"I'm not in the mood," I say. "I'll go sit somewhere else. You can get used to what it will be like when I am married and you're left behind by yourself."

I push myself up on the edge of the table and put my chair back in place.

"Susanna! Stay here!" says my mother in a whisper. "Sit down!"

Sit! Stay! Eat!

"Bark at someone else," I say.

I squeeze between the chairs. I don't get very far because a voice thunders out over the loudspeakers, welcoming everyone and promising us all a fabulous party.

The people around me slide their chairs away from the tables, and I'm suddenly caught between clapping hands and jabbing elbows. Plates are being piled up everywhere, knives and forks are being collected. Anyone who hasn't finished has to stand guard over their food. Activity takes the square by storm and whips it into white water. Because the party is starting, yes, the party's really starting up now, with pounding music and colored lights painting the tent blue and yellow and red.

"And who will it be? Who is going to break the ice this year with the first dance?" shouts the music man into the microphone. Suggestions are offered from left and right. Names, all kinds of names, even old David's up at his attic window. But no Edith, not once.

No Susanna.

"The Reverend ... !" calls the music man. The rest of his joke is drowned out by almost hysterical cheering, because Father Drecht has appeared in the red, yellow, blue light on the dance floor.

He makes a gesture that's supposed to calm everyone down, but the opposite happens, the cheers get even louder. He's relishing his success. His face is radiant. He searches the front rows for a partner and finally settles on Lily, provoking a new round of applause.

Lily stands there quivering like a bird and doesn't recover until she hears the first notes of a polka, a polka she recognizes. She takes Father Drecht's hands, waits two beats, then dances gracefully over the gleaming floor. Around and around, as if she and the priest are intent on checking out every dark corner the tent has to offer.

Everyone on the square is clapping along to the beat. Including Wolf. He's standing now, with his legs slightly spread, and I deliberately adopt the same posture. Smile the way he's smiling.

"Don't forget to change partners!" shouts the music man.

Father Drecht is having the time of his life. As if the polka has taken over his head and his legs, he skips in a half-circle to Amanda, who crows and pats her chest, splutters objections, then sways off with him anyway.

The dance floor fills to continual cries of "Change partners!" The first polka fades into another. The tent is bursting with music and voices and stamping feet. The air is cooler behind me than it is in front of me.

My mother is nowhere in sight and—more upsetting—neither is Wolf. I peer over my shoulder, his spot on the steps is empty, as if he was never even there.

Suddenly I feel hands on my butt and a gut against my stomach.

"So, Susanna, not dancing?" Wester presses against me and lifts me up. He drags me toward the tent, knocking two chairs over in the process, one of which crashes against my leg. He puts me down again between the bouncing bodies as if he's planting a potato and spins me around at least ten times in a row. It's making me giddy. He stinks of sweat, he stinks of beer, he stinks of grease from the barbecue.

"You're such a sweet young thing, if I squeezed you you'd break," he slobbers in my ear. "I could snap you with my bare hands."

"No bones in my butt," I say.

"And again!" screams the music man.

New hands grab me immediately.

"You had him already as well, the octopus!" shouts Walda.

We waltz past Wester, that's right, we waltz, because as far as I can tell nobody is dancing to the music anymore. We have to go with the flow, the dance floor is packed. Walda giggles with every thump she gets.

"Thanks for your help this afternoon!" she yells in my ear.

"Don't start!"

"What?"

"Forget it!" Words are pointless. Scream and holler, that's what you have to do.

"You didn't stick around long!" Walda throws her

head back, hangs on my shoulders with all her weight, and cracks up as though she's just told a dirty joke.

"And again!"

"Here, here's my mother!"

That bitch, I think, and Carla falls into my arms. She's gone completely wacko. There's an almost lecherous gleam in her eyes, her forehead is shiny with beads of sweat.

"Susanna!" she screams. "Susanna, I can't take anymore!"

Yes you can, yes you can, flashes through my mind, and I start spinning in circles. Faster, faster, faster, faster. Carla shrieks. Yellow. Red. Blue. The light flashes in my face. The colors are making me sick. But Carla just roars with laughter, she laughs like a lunatic.

"And again!"

She lets go, and I fly out of her arms, falling splat on the floor between the dancing bodies. Someone kicks me in the side, someone stands on my hand, I scream with pain. I scramble up, lashing out with my arms, getting another thump from the left, another kick from the right. Someone grabs my wrists and pulls me toward them, then immediately lets go.

In the same instant, the music drops. The movement around me stops. The light turns red, mainly red, and saxophone glides out of the speakers. Around me, laughing and puffing people are leaving the dance floor. I feel like someone has pulled a plug and the crowd is literally flowing out of the tent. Only a few couples are left. They swirl around me like water. One ripple is bigger than the rest and washes up against me: Wolf. He doesn't notice me. He's dancing with Walda.

Numbed, I stand among the dancing couples. Teased-up hairdos and red faces block my view and leave me twisting my neck to catch a glimpse of Wolf and Walda. They're not kissing. The whole time, I keep on thinking, they're not kissing, because that's what the lyrics of this slow number are all about.

After five verses describing a broken heart, a female singer sings of red lips and passionate love on the beach of Malaga. That rhymes with "la la la."

"Looking for a man?" asks Amanda in passing. Her voice carries like a bell, even Wolf looks up.

At last. He's taken aback, that's obvious.

I elbow through the couples. Don't follow me, I think, just stay where you are, I'm already leaving. I scrap that idea right away, because out of the corner of my eye I see him coming toward me. He takes my hand—I almost hold it out to him—and whispers something I can't quite understand. He says it with a questioning look in his eye, though, so I automatically say, "Yes."

"Great," he answers, and puts his arms around me, and the beach of Malaga suddenly rhymes with "my heart is true and I love you."

He has soft arms—I can feel every inch of them on my skin—and he's warm and smells good.

"I need you," I whisper.

Surprised, he holds me a bit farther away and frowns.

"I mean, I want to ask you something."

"Now?"

"They'll hear us."

"With music this loud?"

"You never know."

He moves his hands a little higher up my back. One finger brushes the back of my neck. The hairs there all stand up.

"Alright," he says. "Where?"

"Dunno," I say. "Behind the church?"

"When?"

"Soon. In half an hour. They'll be getting everything ready for the summer bonfire." I nod at the open spot between the tables, where branches and bits of timber are piled up and a can of gasoline is waiting.

"A fire," says Wolf. "Fantastic." He pulls me closer and buries his nose in my hair. "It's a deal," he whispers.

NINE

Behind the church, the moon is lying on its back. The gravestones are patches in the grass, like sheets someone has forgotten to bring in. Wolf is standing in the semi-darkness under the linden trees, up against the wall of the annex. His face lights up orange in the glow of his cigarette, and for those few seconds I know for sure that he's looking in my direction.

The music on the square sounds farther away than it is, almost as if it's coming down from the sky. They've started the voyage-around-the-world. The men have rolled up their pants, the women are swishing their skirts, and they're all trying to out-scream each other—that's their idea of Texas. Afterward they'll dance a habanera in Havana, and kick up their legs in Paris. They'll waltz together in Vienna, and do a few more dances that remind them of some country or other. It's the same every year.

I try to shut out everything except the wind rustling in the lindens. Carefully, I pick out a path between the gravestones, then sit down silently next to Wolf.

I look at him. He looks at me, takes a last puff of his cigarette, and stubs it out against the wall. Slowly he breathes out.

"We don't need to whisper," I say.

"We haven't whispered anything yet," he answers.

I chuckle softly, then I'm quiet again. We don't need to whisper anything either, that's fine by me. I'm happy just sitting here, even with the chill of the earth crawling up my legs. Mosquitoes buzz around my head, they're doing a voyage-around-the-world in the air.

"You wanted to talk to me," says Wolf.

He plucks a blade of grass and lets it slip slowly through his fingers. He plucks another, and another, then he tries to braid them.

"This afternoon I acted kind of—uh—funny," I say.

"Not really," he says, without looking up from the braid. "I didn't give it another thought."

"Oh!"

I have to take a deep breath. I hadn't counted on him saying something like that. The mosquito dance party has moved down to my throat, they've picked up the sweet smell of blood.

Wolf lets the braid slip through his fingers and stares at his empty hands. The silence goes to my head. Say something, I think. You're the oldest, it's up to you, say something.

"But you wanted to talk to me," he says suddenly. He follows it up with a yawn. Little girls who want to talk to him bore him.

"Forget it," I say. I've stopped thinking that he'll be able to help me work it all out. Someone who forgets so fast and yawns so easily isn't the person to help you think things through.

I swat at the mosquitoes and almost jump up, but manage to restrain myself just in time. I don't want to leave. Who else have I got to talk to? Nobody. I pretend I'm just getting more comfortable. I can't bring myself to look at him.

"You've come this far. You can't say A without saying B," I hear him say.

I draw a letter B in the grass.

"B," I say.

He doesn't say anything. He acts like he's waiting for the whole alphabet, then suddenly touches my shoulder.

"Come on, Susanna," he says.

I shiver. On his lips my name sounds beautiful. Almost like a breeze, but a very gentle one. My name glides past my throat, down my back.

"Come on, Susanna," I say.

He thinks I'm joking, smirks, and shakes me by the arm, "Tell me."

It takes a while for me to get a grip on myself. All I really want to do is lay my head on his shoulder and tell him that I'm not in the mood for jokes. But I go straight to the point. My own question is so direct it shocks me. Up till now it's a question I haven't even asked myself in my thoughts.

"What I told you this afternoon," I say. "Don't you believe that, er ... people can make it up to each other?"

He catches his breath.

"That's a lot of B," he says. "What do you mean?"

"That's all," I say. "What I mean is, making it up. Making peace, if you like."

"Hallelujah," says Wolf.

"I'm serious. I want ..." What do I want? How in God's name can I go up against the whole village?

"I can't explain," I sigh. To my horror, my hand comes down on his leg and I jerk it back up, but he lays his hand on top of it and says—suddenly deadly serious— "What can you expect in a hornet's nest like this?"

I look for his eyes in the dark. I look for words in my head.

"Hornet's nest?" I say in the end.

He pushes off from the wall and kneels in front of me. For a moment I can only hear the buzzing of the mosquitoes, then everything is there again: the rustling leaves, the music from the sky.

"You get to choose," he says. "Either you poke a hole in the nest with your finger and get stung all over, or else you run away as fast as you can." He bends toward me and whispers, "If I were you, I'd take choice number two. You're on your own, Susanna." He says it slowly and so clearly that the words almost appear before me. You're on your own, Susanna—blown up in big letters on the graveyard wall.

Wolf pats me on the cheek and smiles. "You can't do anything all by yourself. And you know that I can't help you. You don't need me to tell you that. I just blew into town, I don't know anyone, how can I tell you what to do? Up till now I've had fun. I just join in with the rest. Maybe you'd be better off doing the same. Dance. Party. That seems like the best to me. It really does."

He stands up slowly. He doesn't groan and his knees don't creak, and all the force comes out of his legs. He nods down at me from on high. He's inches away from patting me on the head.

"See you in a bit," he says. "Till then," and he disappears into the darkness under the trees. He reappears in the light next to the church, then disappears again around the corner.

A mosquito drills into my ear. The moon's hanging crooked.

TEN

I've just decided to go after Wolf when I spot some light off to one side. Either a light's gone on some-where inside my head, or else something was moving over there.

I scour the graveyard with my eyes, from the oldest, crooked headstones nearby to the new section beyond the lindens where the graves follow the slope, each new row higher than the one before it. I open my eyes wide so that they won't miss a thing, so they'll spot everything in the gloom, in the darkness, and from one moment to the next my arms are covered in goose bumps. I hug myself, but it doesn't help. I hear myself breathing, I hear myself making a noise. Close to the wall on the other side of the graveyard, I see a shadow.

I don't know what shocks me the most. Helen is someone I'd never avoid, Helen is always welcome no matter when she shows up, but seeing her here—on the other side of the village festival, with the voyage-around-the-world coming to an end—makes me step back, clap a hand over my mouth, shake my head.

She's standing at my father's graveside. That's the spot, and Helen's who it is. I could point to that spot with my eyes closed, no matter which direction I was coming from. I could pick Helen out from a thousand silhouettes, I see her often enough and always standing that same way. She'll grow old with a hump, I'd stake my life on it. That's what being weighed down with worry does to your back.

I can't stop the things I'm seeing and hearing and feeling from getting mixed up in my mind. Helen is standing at my father's grave, and I feel that I should be standing there. What do I care about Wolf? What do I care about the village? Until today I couldn't have cared less about the village, but now that my mother's done an about-face, I suddenly feel an urge to belong. What if I went and belonged fully with Helen, with Helen and my father, and let the world turn?

But still I make myself small, I can't help it. I don't want her to see me. I huddle against the wall, scraping my arm because I'm not thinking about what I'm doing, and sit there quietly with my heart trembling in my mouth. I try to think straight, but can't. The heat and the dark belong together. I can't keep the noise over there separate from the silence here. I wish I could take another step back and get away from myself, but I know that's impossible. I belong with myself, that's what I should be thinking, but inside my head, Wolf only has to whisper once that I'm alone, and my shoulders are drooping already.

A strange sadness comes up within me. I pout and sigh. The corners of my mouth sag, my cheeks feel like they're bulging, and I breathe out into the darkness. As long as I don't give a name to the haze before my eyes, everything stays simple. Nothing's choking me. I try to shut Wolf up, other-wise it will get so dark here. I'm not alone, I repeat to myself while cautiously following the wall away from the party and away from Helen. Every move I make is as slow as the air moving through the lindens. I've got time to think about where I'm putting my feet and how I'm holding my hands, and I don't take my eyes off Helen for a second. She's bowed before the grave, praying the way I never do, talking to my father the way I do every day. When I reach the corner of the annex and Helen disappears out of sight, I catch myself talking out loud. I say, "Bye-bye, Daddy."

Around the corner it suddenly feels like there's no party going on anywhere. Helen no longer exists.

I press my warm back against the cool wall and close my eyes. I try to think of something happy.

I see the whole village before me on a peaceful spring day. Everyone's being nice to each other. And especially nice to Helen. Carla is in her kitchen baking waffles, Walda's being friendly, my mother's beaming. The valley has been awash with peace for days on end, the orchard's a cloud of blossom, and my father's still alive. And me, I'm bright and beautiful. Everything is good and different from now.

Isn't it?

I should have kept my eyes shut. From where I'm standing, I can see the orchard. Without a single blossom. The cheerful village in my head smells like sausages, not waffles. You can't change things by thinking them different.

I stand there for a long time staring at the dark orchard. I stand there so long with my thoughts dangling like loose threads in my mind that in the end I can't remember which ones I've tied together. I hold on tight to the last thread. It's called Rudy.

I sneak a look around the corner of the annex. Helen is still standing there in the company of my father. I listen to the distant noises. Using those snatches of music to check that it's true, that I really don't want to dance and really don't want to party. Until I know for sure: I wouldn't go back to that party, not if they paid me.

I'm alone, and I'm going to do something.

I take a first step. And a second. A third.

ELEVEN

Behind the houses, a dome of light is hanging over the square, and above the kennel it's dark. At the end of the road through the apple trees, the floor lamp is on inside the house. I see the corner of an open newspaper beneath it and sigh all the air out of my lungs. Rudy is home.

The dogs start up the moment they smell and hear me. They're even noisier than the music and voices in the distance, and behind the window the newspaper crumples. But not for long. The newspaper goes back up, the light plays on the paper as Rudy turns the page. Why should he pay the dogs any mind? He's expecting Helen.

I wipe the sweat from the back of my neck. My hand is almost as clammy as the hot spot under my hair. My arms are glistening. My legs, too. It's hard to walk in the muggy heat. My glistening left leg takes the first step, my glistening right leg follows, and I try to find a rhythm that suits the way I feel. It has to be fast, very fast. I'm breathing deeply—deep breaths in and out—and keeping my eye on the front door, watching it get bigger and come closer.

I concentrate on the trembling finger I hold out to the doorbell. I prepare myself for the sound of the bell and the light I will soon be standing in. The bell is loud, the bell goes with Rudy, and I'm glad that the noise makes the dogs bark even louder. The light above the front door switches on, the light is bright, the light goes with Rudy as well, and I deliberately look over at the dogs, so that I can be a different person when I turn back to look at Rudy when he appears in the doorway. I see his big head, his broad shoulders. I can't stand the man, but I smile with a mask I've borrowed from my mother.

"Sorry, Rudy," I say. "Sorry for disturbing you so late, but I just had to, it had to be now. The party's on and I talked to Mom and—oh, I'm not explaining it properly."

Rudy doesn't say a word. He stands there with the doorknob in one hand and his paper in the other, look-ing at me with a bored expression—no, not even bored, the man hardly has feelings at all, let alone ones that show on his face.

"What do you want?" he says, just to make me stop flapping my hands and rocking back and forth.

"A dog," I blurt, exactly the way I would if I had really been promised a dog. I'm not lying, I'm just skipping a few years. "I've talked about it with Mom before, Rudy, sometimes I've talked about before with

Mom, about Daddy promising me a dog in the old days, ages ago, and now and then we talk about it, like now, and now it's okay."

"Stand still, girl. Speak clearly. Stop raving. You're getting on my nerves. Whatever you want, ask Helen. She's not here. She said she didn't want to miss that party of yours."

"My mother thought I should ask you, Rudy, not Helen."

"Ask me what?" He raises his voice. Usually I'd shrink, but now it only makes me stand taller.

"Whether you've got a litter right now," I say, as if I don't know. I beam as broadly as I can. "And whether I can choose a pup."

Rudy shuts his mouth and thinks. I can tell he's thinking money. What does he care about pups? As long as the cash bell rings.

"And it has to be now?"

I nod my head. I nod again, harder. "Now," I say. "Mom agreed now, she's finally agreed to the dog Daddy promised me, and who knows, tomorrow she might say no again. 'Nope, changed my mind,' that's what she'll say, so please, Rudy, come on down to the square, don't give Mom a chance to back out of it."

Rudy lets go of the doorknob.

"She can come up here herself. Fix it up with Helen."

"But she always says that you do the money side. Please!"

Rudy is silent. He looks down at the newspaper in his hands, at the slippers on his feet, he looks back at his torture when the master goes by. They whine. They yelp as if their lungs are being squished flat and all the sound has to come out at once. In the middle of all the racket, Rudy shouts something back over his shoulder. Something about paying, paying first, that's what I decipher from the syllables I can make out, and he doesn't look like he's planning on repeating himself. He bangs his hand on one of the metal gates and walks on. The rattling passes into the other cages, the metal vibrates. The dogs hurl themselves against the bars, as if one day they'll find the strength to burst right through and follow their master.

I nod at Rudy, though he's long stopped looking. The smile on my face is no longer part of a mask. I smile with pride: all by myself I have succeeded in sending Rudy somewhere he hasn't been for years. He's walking blindly into his undoing. As long as everyone down there does their bit to help.

My smile gets even wider when I turn back to the litter. Three pups are sitting together in the straw like a picture postcard. A fourth pup has been trying to pick a fight with a rag, but now he turns his back on it and starts wagging his tail. If I could choose a puppy, this is the one I'd choose. I knew it the moment I saw him. Panting and laughing at the same time, he comes over to the low wall and stands up against it. Any other day would see me bend over toward him. My hands would start petting even before they felt his fur. But not now.

In my mind I see the square. I float above the tent, waiting for Rudy. I'm the only one who knows that he's easy chair. He's not coming. His whole body is telling me so. He's already shaking his head.

"I've got a litter," he says suddenly. "A litter of four." He disappears behind the door, then reappears without the newspaper and with his shoes on and a bunch of keys in one hand. "It's a good litter. It won't come cheap."

I scrunch up my eyebrows and let the corners of my mouth sag as if I really have no idea how much pedigreed dogs can cost, and look around as if I don't know this house, either, and am wondering where they keep the puppies.

"Stand still, will you?" says Rudy again, but I think I can already hear a gentler tone creeping into his voice. He knows well enough that I can't stand still if I have to walk to the kennel at the side of the house with him. I hear puppies whining, and I start acting like I'm whining myself as well.

"Oh, Rudy, so nice of you, Rudy," I say, and he unlocks the door, flicks on the shed light, and hands me the keys. He doesn't even glance at the litter. He turns his head away and asks whether he'll be able to find my mother in the crowd.

"She's sitting down," I say. "She's not dancing. She's sitting more or less at our front door. Oh, thank you, Rudy."

"Alright, already," he says. "Lock up when you're finished. Leave the keys in the house." He doesn't say good-bye, he turns his broad back on me and walk off. The instant the dogs catch wind of him, their cage are too small. Such a small space with so many bars halfway through the orchard, and I'm already enjoying the changing expressions. My mother is still sitting on her chair, of course. She wants to get away from all the noise—back to her spot on the couch or to bed with an ice pack—but she's thinking, I'll stay a little bit longer. In a few seconds she'll see Carla seize her opportunity when Rudy appears on the square. The trick with the finger and the hornet's nest. Getting Helen is half measures, but with Rudy, Carla can go gunning for the head culprit. Hello, Rudy. How are the dogs, Rudy? You still dare to show your face, Rudy?

The kennel is virtually silent. The litter of four is looking up at me. Like me, they seem to be holding their breath and listening to the silence. They're waiting for me to move.

Rudy must be reaching the village square right about now. Carla sees him first. She flashes a message to Walda—her eyes can do that—and Walda tells Amanda. In a few seconds the news has spread. "There he is! Look, there he is! What a nerve! He has the gall to come down here!"

I notice my fist is clenched so hard it hurts. At first I'm just standing there watching the picture in my head, then I see where the pain is coming from. A big key has left an imprint in my hand. It's the biggest key of the whole bunch, the master key that unlocks every cage. In the same instant I see Carla's face reddening, I see her mouth opening, her trembling hand pointing at Rudy—no, not at Rudy, at a big, black yapping beast.

I jump because the puppies jump. They jump because I suddenly start moving, turning off the light above their box, shutting the door, changing my walk to run. Yes, I say to myself. The fool has given me the key. The biggest key. The key that unlocks every cage. I take it between my thumb and index finger and hold it up. I've seen how it works often enough. One key for all the cages, one turn to the right, and they can really start to party down there on the square. The dogs will still be able to smell which direction the fool took, they'll be able to follow him. Catch up to him even. Give them even more reason to go at him down there on the square. Dares to come here and brings his dogs with him! What an outrageous scandalous nerve the man has! Knock the smile off his face!

The dogs can't stand the jingling keys. I don't belong in this yard. They leap up, flying at the light. Their mouths open and shut, open and shut, and a dull noise comes out from between their jaws. They're snapping at me to hurry. They're saying, "Now!"

Now!

I only see one cage, the first. That dog can be the first to go. It barks the loudest, it jumps the highest, and inside its cage it snaps wildly in every direction. Maybe it will have another chance to snap in every direction soon. Carla will have her punishment as well, a bleeding leg. The dog wants out. To be on its way. Maybe it doesn't even want to follow its master. Maybe it doesn't want to sink its fangs into a leg. It puts its paws up on the gate and pants in my face.

"Okay, boy," I say. "Good boy, you can go, boy." With one sure movement, I shove the key into the lock, turn it, pull open the gate. The bang of the opening gate makes me shut my eyes. In a flash I think that I might be the one the dog bites, but the animal is overcome with happiness. Yapping, it hurtles down the path between the cages, it comes back, it changes its mind, it almost does a somersault in midair, then shoots off, heading for the orchard.

In my mind I keep count as it bounds down the path. How long will it take to reach the square? Is it coincidence that I hear cheering in the distance? I curse myself for not being able to look and listen at the same time. Now! Now! Around me there is nothing but noise. My head is full of it, it feels numb from the heat. I can't control my hands. The key is shaking, jangling against the lock of the next cage. The keyhole is too small, the hole is crooked, the key doesn't fit. I swear loudly, and the swearing suddenly makes the key fit. When the gate swings open, a strange noise comes out of my throat, more fright than relief, because the dog throws itself up against me on its way out, knocking me back and into the bars. It smears a trail of drool over my arm, falls over, jumps up again, and tears off down the path. All the dogs are barking at each other and at me. They don't think I'm fast enough. They want to go to the square. My head is pounding from all their nowing, all their whining. My ears are buzzing. All the other noises are far away. I think I catch the sound of people cheering again. Or is that the dogs? Is it howling more than cheering? Or screaming more than howling?

I rip open my hand on the lock of the next cage, but I don't feel the pain until I see the blood. I tug at the lock, pull open the cage, kick the dog when it's too slow to rush out. The roar in my head is deafening. I see the blood stains on my dress, I see a blur before my eyes. I have time to think, I'm going to fall, but I don't fall. I stumble to the next cage. I hold my good right bleeding hand to my mouth. I taste the iron of my blood, I taste iron from the key, I taste my sweat. My tongue is swollen, my lips are warm. The keys slip out of my awkward hand, and I kick them in my hurry to pick them up. They slide along in the dust, and I'm about to bend over to get them, but I fall backward instead, because someone has grabbed me by the arm and is pulling me along so hard I feel the tug in the muscles of my back. I stumble and spin around but stay on my feet, and I look at the hand holding my hand, and the hand is Helen's, and she makes sure I keep my balance.

"Susanna!" pants Helen, and I hear her, but I only see her mouth move later, and I can see her, but I'm looking at her back. How can I see her mouth moving if she's walking in front of me, pulling me along with her, down the road that leads through the orchard?

"Come here!" she shouts. Her voice sounds shrill, and I think, why's she calling me, I'm already here, and I try to get her attention by tugging at her arm, but she keeps on dragging me along with all her strength.

"Here! Here!" she screams, "Here!" and only then do I realize that she's calling the dogs, and that it's useless. All the noise is coming from the kennel behind us and from the square in front of us, and in between, nothing, nothing rustling the grass, nothing panting between the trees.

"Come here!" screams Helen again. I think she's crying. She stops and pulls me toward her. With her face close to mine, she asks where Rudy is. "Where is he? Have you seen him? If he sees this! Where is he?"

Her voice is shrill, I'm shocked by how shrill it is. I don't know if I can bear it, that's how shrill it is. All I want to do is retrace my steps, take exactly the same steps back again, so that the dogs are back in their cages, and I'm standing in front of the house, and looking in and seeing the light above Rudy and his newspaper, and changing my mind, and quietly returning to the graveyard, and nodding at what Wolf says. I nod, he's right.

Then I wouldn't have to see Helen's panic now. Then I could go and dance. Party. Then I would be alone, but less alone than usual, because Wolf would be with me, and he'd smile at me and leave it to me to choose. You going to come dance? Are you coming back to the party? I can say "no." I can tell him that I want to go to Daddy's grave first, and then Helen and I could talk. I can stay there standing against the wall and spend the whole night building villages where it smells of waffles and rains blossoms.

I look at Helen, I start to gesture that I'm sorry, but I don't know if I am sorry, so I don't make the gesture, and I don't know anything else, I only point with my chin in the direction of the square, because all kinds of things are happening down there.

"There," I say.

Helen jerks around.

"There?" she says, and has to repeat it before she

can believe it. "With the others?"

My head moves slowly up and down, and I feel the blood draining away from my face. Down there on the square they aren't cheering. Suddenly I hear it clearly. Cheering sounds different. They're shouting, but not cheering. The noise blows over in gusts, but that's impossible, there's almost no wind. It's because my heart is pounding in my throat, blocking my ears, drowning out all the other sounds. I break out in a sweat, as if I'm standing in front of a fire. I think I see the ground coming up toward me, but Helen brings me back to the sky. She grabs me by both arms, as if I'm an old coat she wants to look at, and she looks at me, she shakes me, her breath steams out over my face, and a quiet whimper escapes from her throat. How could I do it? How in God's name could I do that?

"Here," she says, "you stay here." She lets go of me, almost making me lose my balance, then runs off, grabbing branches of apple trees along the way as if that's the only way she can keep from falling. She disappears around the bend in the road.

My head moves by itself, I press my hands against my ears, squeeze my eyes shut, and after it's been quieter and darker for a while, and I've imagined Helen rescuing Rudy, I let go of my ears and open my eyes. Even before the image of Helen on the square has had time to fade away, a muffled boom makes me jump. All my muscles tense up at once, my back goes straight as an arrow, and my eyes open wide. Over the square a gray cloud with orange sparks in the middle shoots up into the sky above the orange glow of the summer bonfire. In the old days people would be cheering and singing by now. In the old days they would be dancing around the fire. Now a roar goes up, exploding just like the fire and sounding like it's coming out of just one mouth. The mouth of an entire village, reacting like one man.

TWELVE

I don't know how long I stand there. The buzzing in my head falters, and every time it falters I hear voices and sounds I can't quite place. I try to put faces to the voices, to work out what the sounds are. I can't work out whether the buzzing belongs in my ears, or even if it is buzzing. Whether it's not just the drone of a distant car. There are shouts, the crackling of fire. I look down and see myself. My feet, my legs apart, my arms held out, my fingers spread.

I see blue.

It's not my imagination. It's not a spark in my head, not something moving somewhere and catching the light for a second. The blue light is everywhere, but only now and then, and before I know it, it's disappeared again. My eyes shoot from left to right, in front, behind. A dry pop in my head, and I can hear again. Close by, really close by—it sounds as if I could reach out and touch it—I hear slamming doors and metal on metal. Voices, lots of voices.

Slowly I start moving. As if I have to learn to walk and need to be careful. I could fall any minute now.

The blue light has reached the village square. It's turning. Blue roofs, blue steeple, blue trees. An engine starts. Whining like a delivery truck, a car drives off. I hear the engine taking the curves in the road. Into the distance, the blue light colors trees, buildings, signposts. The sound of the engine merges into other sounds.

I keep on moving. Slowly, because I have to concentrate on what I'm doing. I walk through the darkest patches on the path, because then I know that I'm walking through the darkest patches on the path. After that, the streetlight colors my arms orange, and then I say what color my arms are, orange. I cross my arms against the cold that suddenly hits me. I hug myself tight and keep on moving. If I stop for just a moment, then I think too much. Then the first things that come to mind are the most horrible. Carla's face is bleeding. She's sitting on a chair with her legs out and her head back. Walda's hands and arms are covered with bandages, and she's got a fat lip from a punch in the face, but she's still on her feet, though I can tell she's feeling groggy and would rather lie down. She's crying, I think. I can't stop thinking. Even when I start walking faster, I can't shake off the images. At our house my mother has collapsed on our doorstep. Her face is red, her eyes are puffy, she's run out of tears. Her hand is resting on Helen's knee. Helen is sitting on a chair in front of her, leaning forward, holding her hands to her face, rocking back and forth with misery. She can't cry, she's forgotten how. She can make the noise, but the tears don't come.

In the end I've made myself so scared that it takes me ages to get up the courage to go on. I'm standing in the darkness at the side of Carla's house. One step and the square will be in front of me.

The only words I can think of are dark and dismal. Blood. Punishment. Hate. Rage. Pain.

I take a deep breath and shuffle forward, looking down. No one calls my name. No one lashes out. I see that your mind plays tricks on you. Brains can't be trusted. Nothing I imagined is true.

Lights are shining from behind the doors and windows of all the houses on the square. Inside, people are standing together. They gesture, point outside. The square itself has been through a war. Chairs and even tables have been knocked over. The tent on the lawn is dark. The bonfire crackles, flaring up every now and then with a gust of wind. It's giving off a heat you can feel and see all over the square. The fronts of the houses shimmy with its glow. Nobody is looking at the fire. Everyone's giving the fire the cold shoulder. Pretty soon it will go out by itself. Tomorrow there will be a pile of ash.

Near Amanda's store, groups of people are standing around talking, or sitting around tables. Wester is the focus of one, Lily is in another, farther along Dr. Bock is explaining something to Father Drecht.

"He asked for it," I hear nearby. I look to the side and up. Walda and Carla are standing on Carla's balcony with a few other people. Carla has her back turned to me and seems bigger than the others. Someone says it went too far and that nobody could stop it, and someone else says that violence never solves anything, but it was good, good, very good that his wife showed up when she did, and Carla keeps on shaking her head firmly, and says again, "He asked for it, the pigheaded fool, and they're in it together."

I'm expecting someone to turn around at any moment and point at me. I can already hear the question, "Where have you been?" But nobody notices me. Nobody makes a connection between a bunch of dogs and Susanna Dantine who disappeared from the world for about an hour. Only Helen knows better, but she's nowhere in sight. I see her frightened face before me, when she asked me where Rudy was.

I take a few steps onto the square and look around cautiously. Three dogs are lying down at the top of the church steps. They're tied to the railing, and all three of them are looking in the same direction.

First I wonder who tied them up there, then I wonder what they're looking at, and look with them, searching so hard for something moving that I overlook Wolf. He's standing at the bottom of the steps, about to sit down on his scooter. He doesn't need to watch what he's doing. He can watch me as long as he likes. Long, longer than necessary, he looks in my direction.

I nod at him.

He smiles briefly, then wryly, and nods back. By looking at the dogs, then back at me, he shows me without words that he knows what I did. I answer by nodding again. I don't mind him knowing. He's different.

He holds up one hand and puckers his lips. Silently I catch the kiss.

I'm the only one who doesn't jump from the racket the scooter suddenly makes. The others are startled, they turn around and hold their hands to their chests. The dogs jump up, straining at the rope and barking at the noise.

Wolf doesn't look up or around. You can see that he doesn't belong here. He wobbles between the tables on his scooter, hunches over a little, and disappears down the street he came up this afternoon.

I listen to the noise dying away, brushing my lips with my fingers to feel his kiss.

"So," I whisper.

I stroll between the tables to our house. I set a chair right, pick up a fallen plate that's still in one piece, and look back at the square.

Then I open our front door, very softly. Very softly, I close our front door. The softness is automatic. I take off my shoes and put them next to each other on the mat. I walk barefoot down the hall and up the three steps to my mother's bedroom. She doesn't jump when I come in, and I'm not surprised to see her lying on the bed. I walk around it, to the side that used to be Daddy's, and sit down carefully. I stretch my legs, one after the other, slide up the bed a little, and lie down on my back. Only then do I breathe out.

I haven't made any noise, and it stays quiet for a long time. My mother and I look up at the ceiling. I'm not waiting for her to say something, and she's not waiting for me to say something. We both just lie there soaking up the silence.

Then I hear my mother swallow. She turns her head toward me and says, "His wounds will heal."

I turn my head toward her and nod very carefully. I raise my hand, showing her my wound.

"And this one?" I say.

"Show me," she says.

I slide carefully toward her and snuggle up against her, otherwise she can't see my hand.